THE UNGODLY

THE CURSE OF FORGOTTEN VALLEY

NEIL SATER

WEST KILBRIDE LLC

Cover Design by James, GoOnWrite.com

Library of Congress Control Number: 2026902362

ISBN: 979-8-9885508-6-0 (Paperback) | 979-8-9885508-7-7 (eBook)

Published by: West Kilbride LLC 6618 Morningside Dr. Cleveland OH 44141

First edition - 2026

Sign up for Neil Sater's newsletter through his website:

https://authorsater.com/

For my awesome kids, Ian and Kerry
With all my love, from your proud father

Contents

Chapter 1

If only I had listened to Mom.

When everything went horribly wrong, that's what I kept thinking. But the more she resisted my backpacking trip idea, the more determined I was to do it. So yeah, my stubborn streak became my undoing, you could say.

But I'm getting ahead of myself.

"Great. Another buggy," Mom said when we rounded a bend in the road, braking as she approached it.

Bluey, who was sitting on the back seat between my brothers, stuck his head between Mom and me, thinking he might be missing something important. Dustin and Xavier named him Bluey after their favorite cartoon character at the time, even though he's a golden retriever.

"It's just another Amish buggy," I told him while patting his head.

He lay back down, like he understood.

In Homer County, the Amish are a common sight. This latest buggy was crawling slowly up a long hill, which blocked our view of any oncoming cars. If I were driving, I would've squeezed through, but Mom waited, so I rolled my eyes and kept my mouth shut. After the last two buggies, it was clear she wasn't going to listen to me.

When she finally passed it at the top of the hill, I couldn't help but peek at the driver. An Amish man with the usual long gray beard, round-rimmed glasses, and a straw hat lifted his hand in a stone-faced wave, as if I were just the latest in a steady stream of gawking city folk.

Caught in my nosiness, I responded with a disinterested wave and pretended to be watching the countryside.

Focusing on the view was all I could do to suppress my anxious feelings. Mostly farmland, separated by occasional patches of forest, the scenery *was* peaceful-looking. But after a while, it all started to look the same.

"It should be coming up on the right," Mom said a few minutes later, squinting at the navigation map on her phone.

"Welcome to Moravian Village," I said, reading the roadside sign aloud as we passed it. *Strange name,* I thought, wondering where it came from. But yeah, that was where we'd start our hike: outside Moravian Village, Homer County, Ohio.

"So, we're here?" Dustin asked from the back seat. Xavier raised his head from his game console and looked around.

"Almost," Mom answered, slowing down.

As we both scanned the area in search of the trailhead's roadside pull-off, the tassel from my recent high school graduation cap swung from the rearview mirror, its gold charm spelling out "2025."

"Is that it?" I asked, pointing ahead.

Mom nodded, and I heard her suck in a stuttering breath. When she turned into the gravel parking area, my throat tightened. The memory of the last time I'd been here struck me hard. Mom was dropping us off at the same spot where she'd dropped me and Dad seven years prior.

Now, Dad could no longer walk.

I ran a finger over the red silicone bracelet on my other wrist, tracing the contoured letters: "ALS Awareness - Let's Find a Cure!"

Almost two years had passed since Dad's diagnosis. People with ALS, or Lou Gehrig's disease, steadily lose control of their muscles, and many eventually die because they can no longer breathe. What a way to go: trapped in a body that can't even inhale.

So, that's what he was heading for. Dad had the most horrible condition imaginable, and we were all helpless witnesses to his gut-wrenching decline. The doctors didn't expect him to make it another year.

Nurse Donna was currently at the house with him, since he needed constant care these days. In the past month, they put him on a feeding tube. He couldn't even swallow correctly anymore, and if he were to inhale food, he'd have a whole slew of other problems.

As Mom nudged the car up against the brush, she sighed, which came through in a shudder, telling me she, too, was thinking about how so much had changed since the last time we'd been here.

"This is it?" Dustin asked in a disappointed tone.

I didn't dignify his question with a response.

"Emma?" he pressed.

I still didn't answer. Ever since I first suggested the backpacking idea, the twins had their sights set on the Appalachian Trail—the AT, as hikers call it. But I only agreed to take them on the condition that we hike the Buckeye Trail instead. The Buckeye Trail—the BT—is a giant loop, about two-thirds the length of the AT, but all within the state of Ohio, nicknamed the Buckeye State. Hence, the trail's name.

I was able to map out the exact itinerary of the trip Dad had taken me on when I was the boys' age. Referencing the journal I had kept, I managed to pinpoint each of our camping locations, with Dad helping me fill in a few blanks. That's the weird thing about ALS: his mind still works, but he was struggling to speak, so it was getting harder to understand him.

Once I had all those details worked out, that clinched it. We'd hike a one-hundred-mile section in the eastern portion of the state over eight days. This region is pretty countryside, remote and rugged, the Appalachian foothills.

Don't get me wrong, I understood why Mom didn't like the idea of her eighteen-year-old daughter taking her eleven-year-old brothers out on their own. Surprisingly, Dad was okay with it, but with him bedridden and having a hard time even talking, he didn't get much say in such matters anymore. His main stipulation was that I carry a pocket gun in case we ran into any crazy hillbillies—or their crazy dogs. Dad was looking forward to hearing our report. Maybe in a way, he was taking one last adventure through us.

What I couldn't get Mom to understand was that the trip was part of my process of coming to grips with the pending loss of my father. That trip with Dad? Without a doubt, it was my most memorable father-daughter experience.

On *this* trip, the boys were the same age as I had been. Not only would this be therapeutic for me, but I was giving them a piece of what Dad had given me. And with me starting college soon, this was our best chance. Mom reluctantly gave in, under Dad's condition that I carry that handgun.

My skin turned sticky the instant I climbed out of the car into the heat. Just our luck: we'd somehow picked the hottest and muggiest day of the summer to start our journey.

We met behind the car, waiting for the hatch to open so we could lug out our backpacks. "I'll get a photo of you at the trail marker,"

Mom said, pointing at the little sign with the blue blazes marking the trailhead.

I choked up, thinking about how many times I'd looked at the photo Mom took of Dad and me at this same point seven years ago. Shouldering my pack, I headed that way, followed by the twins.

After snapping several photos, Mom gave us all a round of hugs and kisses. As she tugged at Bluey's leash and turned toward the car, I noticed tears running down her cheeks.

I knew it wasn't just the goodbye causing her to cry. The slow process of losing Dad was as draining on her as it was on any of us. Maybe worse.

Me? I fought back the tears, determined to make the occasion joyous for my brothers.

Joyous. Yeah, right.

I had no clue how twisted things would soon get.

CHAPTER 2

The brutal heatwave was the worst part of that day's hike, although the relentless mosquitoes were a close second. They always seem to go hand in hand, don't they?

My brothers didn't seem bothered by either one, though. I'm not sure why the heat didn't get to them, but the mosquitoes were too busy making a meal out of me.

I was grateful when the blue blazes showed the trail crossing a single-lane state roadway, then continuing down what had once been a gravel driveway. We were approaching the nature preserve where we'd spend our first night.

In the overgrowth lining the trail, I spotted a fallen, wooden sign with *CAMP TIMBERWOOD* barely visible across it. Now parkland, the property had once been a Girl Scout campground.

After we trudged past a few boarded-up cabins, the trail thinned. I had worried I might overlook our camping site, but when a clearing came into view off to the side, I immediately recognized it.

"Hey, come back," I yelled to the twins, wiping my sweaty forehead with my shirt's short sleeve. They had been outpacing me all day, despite having joined me on only one of the half-dozen training hikes I took before the trip. So much for my warnings about blisters and sore muscles.

"You passed it." I pointed to the overgrown meadow, about the size of a football field. The twins spun around and headed back to where I stood.

A mosquito buzzed in my ear while I waited for them, so I swatted it away, pulled the repellent out of my pocket, and gave myself a few fresh squirts.

"We're camping *here*?" Xavier asked as he approached, his face twisted in confusion. Apparently, he had imagined something more idyllic than this unkempt clearing.

"Yup, in that level area over there," I said, pointing to where Dad and I had pitched our tent seven years ago.

"What's that swamp?" Dustin asked, pointing beyond the flat area.

"It's a pond," I said. It was tiny—not much bigger than a volleyball court.

"Why's it all scummy?"

"That's..." I stared at the lime-green aquatic plants covering the entire surface, trying to recall the name Dad had used for it. "...duckweed."

A loud croak came from that direction.

Xavier raised his eyebrows. "Was that a cow?"

I laughed. The deep foghorn call *did* sound a lot like a cow mooing. "It's a bullfrog. I remember hearing them when I camped here with Dad."

Dustin scanned our surroundings warily. "It's kind of creepy here."

Neither of us responded to that. Xavier probably didn't want to admit it. I couldn't exactly argue the point myself. I hadn't thought of it as creepy when Dad and I camped here. Then again, I had him to protect me. And that was before I started watching slasher films.

I pushed the idea aside, leaped over the little stream beside the trail, and set off for the flat patch, picking my way through the narrow stretch of brush. My brothers followed close behind.

The twins had been enthusiastic about practicing pitching their tent in our backyard, so theirs was up in half the time it took mine. They weren't quite as useful when it came to gathering firewood, though.

After dinner, I cached our food in a tree, and we spread out on the ground, circling the campfire. Although the sun had dropped low in the sky, it was still hot, so we didn't need to sit near a fire. Except that's what you do when you're camping.

"I'm beat," I told them, checking the time on my phone. "It'll be getting dark soon."

I expected they would whine about the hint I dropped, but neither complained. We'd covered thirteen miles, so they were probably a little worn out, too.

Dustin pulled his burning stick out of the campfire and waved it at me. "Tell us a ghost story."

"Yeah!" Xavier said, suddenly losing interest in the steaming grass stems he'd laid over the hot coals.

I knew delaying bedtime played some part in their request, but it wasn't dark enough for bed, anyway. The bigger issue was whether telling a scary story was a good idea. "You're not going to have nightmares, are you?"

They both shook their heads, but their faces didn't look so convinced. I decided if I was going to do this, I'd better make it a mild one.

"Hmm," I said as I tried to figure out what story I could come up with. I briefly considered searching for something on my phone, since I had service here. But I had left my power bank at home to save weight in my backpack, and since I would have no way to charge my phone before the next day's state park campground, I needed to save my battery.

I thought about telling them about some of the local legends that kids always shared in middle school. The Kirtland Melonheads came to mind, along with the area in the national park they call Helltown. Those disjointed pieces of folklore aren't stories with a clear beginning and ending, though, so I decided they wouldn't work.

"Okay, I've got a good one for you," I eventually declared, switching my gaze slowly between my suddenly attentive brothers. "This is called 'The Troll Skull.' Once upon a time, there was a newlywed couple named Ian and Shannon."

I was telling them a variation of a short story I wrote for my senior year's creative writing class. It was a perfect fit for this moment because the story took place during the couple's honeymoon, which just so happened to be a backpacking adventure on the Buckeye Trail.

"Everything was going great until tragedy struck on the first night."

Xavier and Dustin's eyebrows shot up, and they quit playing with the fire.

"Of course, with it being their honeymoon, they did the nasty in their tent." I knew they'd already learned about this stuff from kids at school. Thank God for elementary schoolyard education.

"Ew." The twins said it in perfect unison, although I heard a tone of intrigue. They would have loved to hear the details, but I had no intention of giving them that thrill.

"While they were 'consummating their marriage' (I used Mom's trick of wrapping air quotes around the term with my fingers), a rattlesnake snuck into their tent."

The twins' faces took on the disturbed look I was hoping for.

I let the tension soak in for a while before continuing. "When they finished banging, Ian heard a rattling sound, and when Shannon moved, the snake struck her in the leg."

My brothers stared at me with their jaws hanging open.

Dustin scanned the nearby ground. "Are there rattlesnakes in Ohio?"

"No," I said firmly. In truth, having researched it, I knew there were two species, but both were extremely rare. My brothers didn't need to know about this fact, though.

"Ian grabbed his knife and cut off the snake's head." I paused for dramatic effect. "But before he could even call 911, it was too late."

"She died?" Xavier just couldn't accept it.

Dustin didn't ask the same question, but it was written on his face.

I nodded grimly. "He checked her breathing, then her pulse. Nothing."

The boys looked crestfallen.

"Ian fell on Shannon, crying for his lost love. He sobbed for an hour, while her body went cold, until he heard a tapping sound outside the tent."

The twins had their eyes fixed on me. Xavier scooched closer to Dustin.

"When Ian peeked out the flap, he saw a hideous little man standing by the dwindling campfire. He was hairy, with a head shaped like a gorilla, warts all over his face, a big nose, and pointy ears. The ugly little man was a troll, and the sound was his walking stick, which he was tapping against the ground. Over his shoulder, he was holding a sack.

"Ian asked, 'What do you want?' The troll put the sack on the ground, then sat beside it. 'I know how much you loved your wife. I came to offer you a way to resurrect her.'

"Ian crawled out of his tent and stood beside the fire. The troll reached into the sack and removed a skull, which also had the shape of a gorilla's head. It was a troll's skull. The troll said, 'Bury your wife with this. It has healing properties.'"

"What's that mean?" Dustin asked.

"It means the skull was magical. It could heal things."

"How?"

"I don't know," I said, a bit irritated. Dustin had a habit of asking too many questions.

Xavier said, "It's a made-up story, Dustin. And anyway, some things can't be explained, you know?"

Dustin frowned and turned to face the fire.

"Anyway, the troll told Ian that if he were to bury Shannon with the skull, in the morning, she would come back to life and crawl out of the grave. Ian stared at the troll, thinking it was too good to be true. The troll tossed the skull to Ian, so on reflex, he caught it. As he rubbed the smooth bone at the top of the skull, the troll said, 'There's only one catch. If you do this, there's a 50-50 chance she'll come back as herself, good as new. But you also have a 50-50 chance she'll come back as one of my kind. The troll stood, turned, and walked off into the dark woods, leaving Ian alone with the skull."

I paused for an intermission, looking up at the sky, darkening on the eastern end. Over at the pond, the bullfrogs were calling in a steady chorus.

"He did it, didn't he?"

I looked at Dustin. Naturally, it was he who had deduced where this was going. Although the twins were identical, Dustin always seemed to be a half step ahead of Xavier when it came to logical reasoning.

I said, "He had to try, right?"

Dustin nodded about this.

"Under the moonlight, Ian used his camping shovel to dig a shallow grave. He laid Shannon in the hole, set the skull on her chest, then covered her with dirt."

My brothers were both gazing at the fire, lost in the emotion of my dark tale.

"When he was finished, Ian said a prayer over Shannon's grave, asking God to bring her back as herself."

I paused, noticing the bullfrogs had gotten louder, then went on with the story.

"Back in the tent, Ian could hardly sleep. He lay there, tossing and turning, sitting up whenever he heard something rustling outside. Half a dozen times, he got up and peeked out. Once, he saw movement by the grave. It turned out to be just a raccoon passing through.

"As he drifted in and out of sleep, Ian wavered between hopefulness and despair. He worried he had made a mistake, and Shannon would come back as an ugly, evil troll."

I drew out those last words, playing up the theatrics. Since I could almost feel the twins' tension, I let that idea simmer. I got up and added a few sticks to the fire, stirring the coals into a strong new flame. Half the sky had darkened, and the first fireflies blinked along the edge of the trees.

After I settled back into place, I continued. "Ian eventually fell asleep shortly before dawn. It was the sound of footsteps that woke him up. He crawled out of his sleeping bag and unzipped his tent flap. He froze, covering his eyes from the blinding sunlight. A shadow fell on him. Shaking in anticipation, he uncovered his eyes. Shannon stood in front of him, as beautiful as ever."

Dustin let out a visible sigh.

Xavier said, "So, she was okay?"

I smiled. "Good as new. Just needed a bath. Almost as much as you guys."

They laughed, like the story's outcome had them breathing easy now. I was proud of myself for giving my tale an uplifting ending. For the audience, I improved it, although some of my creative writing classmates would *hate* this version. I didn't need my brothers having nightmares on this trip, though.

"We need that troll skull for Dad," Dustin said.

A sinking feeling took hold in my gut. I nodded weakly and stared at the fire, avoiding looking at him. What could I say to that?

Xavier sniffed, but added nothing. His silence said everything.

All of a sudden, I was feeling like I had picked the wrong story. I had sugarcoated the story for my brothers, but even *this* version had struck a nerve.

It was a good thing we didn't have that troll skull, though. When you boil it all down, the real version of my story is a cautionary tale, without the happy ending. Driven by his grief, Ian tried to cheat death. He did something reckless and paid dearly for it. There's a lesson in that: desperation can make us do reckless things, and recklessness may not work out well.

The idea of magical healing, though...wouldn't that be nice? Alas, it was nothing but a fairy tale.

I looked up at the sky, which was now mostly dark, and said, "Don't tell Mom I told you a scary story."

"We won't," the boys said together.

That prompted me to pick up my phone. When I touched the screen, it showed I still had one bar of service. I tapped out a text to Mom: "Heading to bed soon. All is well."

Within seconds, she reacted with a heart. We had agreed to keep the calls to a bare minimum, although knowing we'd have service most of the time helped her come around to the backpacking plan.

"It may not seem like it now," I said, tucking my phone into my pocket. "...but you're going to remember this trip your whole life."

"Why?" Dustin asked.

I pushed the stubs of the burned branches into the fire while I considered this, trying to formulate an explanation. "I'm not sure," I admitted. "But things like this stick with you."

I somehow knew it wasn't just the sentimental memories of my father that had made our trip so memorable. Spending that time together gave us a bond. A shared experience. Memories that would last a lifetime—although ALS was cruelly cutting his short.

"Maybe we'll forget all about it when we hike the Appalachian Trail next year," Dustin said. He couldn't get past his suspicions that the BT was a weak substitute for the AT.

I chuckled. "I'm starting college in a few weeks. With any luck, I'll have an internship next summer." Of course, a lot depended on what happened with Dad between now and then. "So, this is it for me, guys."

The bullfrogs went silent so abruptly, it was as if someone flipped a switch.

I'm sure my brothers noticed too, but neither of them said anything. Maybe they didn't want to acknowledge it. Like if they didn't dwell on it, it wouldn't seem so ominous. Or maybe they just didn't think it was a big deal.

But to me, it didn't seem natural. Acting casual to avoid riling them up, I rolled my head around and looked at the duckweed-covered pond, barely visible in the twilight. Although I saw nothing, I kept watching, figuring *something* must have disrupted them. A minute or two later, the bullfrogs started up again, and before long, they were louder than ever.

I was about to let it go anyway when something howled, way off in the woods, tearing my attention away from the bullfrogs. The boys' heads both whipped around to face me. "Was that a wolf?" Dustin asked in an anxious whisper.

Xavier shifted a little closer to Dustin.

"No," I said. "There are no wolves in Ohio anymore. That was a coyote." I knew from school there were no wolves, but the truth was, I wasn't sure what a coyote sounded like. I said it confidently, though, the way adults talk assertively, even when they aren't sure about things.

Dustin asked, "Why did it howl like that?"

I almost said something about it being hungry, but decided against it. "He's making a booty call."

The boys snickered, but they sounded nervous.

We sat there for a while, waiting to hear it again. When we didn't, I rose to my feet and announced, "We have a long hike ahead of us tomorrow. Time to rest up."

Little did I know, we wouldn't be doing any hiking the next day.

CHAPTER 3

As tired as I was, I should've fallen asleep right away. No such luck, though.

The heat was part of it. It was too hot to get inside my sleeping bag, so I lay on top, and even then, my face and neck were still sweating.

Luckily for them, my brothers must've fallen asleep immediately, because they hadn't made a sound since we turned in.

Over at the pond, the bullfrogs were going at it. Their chorus had grown in volume, so by this point, they were deafening—much louder than I remembered from the Dad trip.

What had me more concerned were the rustling sounds coming from the trees where I had cached our food. Dad had taught me to do that so bears wouldn't come looking for it in the tent. There aren't many bears in Ohio anymore, but this was the one part of the state where they *were* occasionally seen.

I lay there, listening to the raucous bullfrogs in one direction, and something trying to get at our cache in the other. It was impossible to relax, thinking about how if a bear got our food, that would be the end of our big hike.

Alone with my thoughts, I lay there on high alert until finally, I couldn't take it anymore. I had to pee anyway, so I pulled on my boots, unholstered the handgun, and grabbed the flashlight.

After slipping outside, I stood beside the still-glowing embers of the campfire, waiting to see if the twins had heard me. They were out cold, though. Not a peep or any sign of movement came from their tent.

I examined my surroundings. Fireflies were flashing throughout the clearing, dimly visible under the nearly full moon. I looked up at the amazing Milky Way. This was the first time I had seen it so clearly since the Dad trip. He'd explained how light pollution from the city hid it from view where we lived. I hadn't thought of pointing it out to my brothers. Then again, it wasn't fully dark when we turned in, so it wouldn't have been this striking yet.

I wandered over to the edge of the woods where I'd hung the food and switched on the flashlight, pointing the beam up to where I had strung the cache.

A pair of green eyes stared at me from the tree, making me recoil. I shifted the pistol into position and released the safety, reminding myself what Dad had told me: this gun was way too small to kill a bear, but the sound of it should help scare it off.

Then another pair of eyes appeared. The first set blinked off, then the second, and soon, I saw two fuzzy shadows scamper down the tree before running off into the woods. Raccoons. Releasing my breath, I reengaged the safety and slipped the gun into my pocket.

I checked the line where I had tied it off on a nearby tree trunk, tugging to make sure the sack was hanging as I'd left it. It was. I considered taking it down and bringing it into my tent since, apparently, bears weren't going after it. Raccoons weren't going to come into my tent. Or would they? Since they hadn't managed to get to the cache after an hour or two of trying, I decided it might be safer to leave it be.

Next, I focused on my restroom duty, stepping further into the woods for privacy in case the twins ventured out. To avoid peeing on my boots, I held onto a small tree and leaned back, cursing the injustice of how easy men had it when it came to doing this in the woods.

The bullfrogs suddenly went silent, leaving only the sound of leaves rustling in the breeze. *That's strange,* I said to myself, but then I remembered the same thing happening before we went to bed, so I didn't give it much thought.

After finishing, I picked my way back through the brush, illuminating my path with the flashlight beam. Just before I stepped into the clearing, another pair of glowing eyes appeared a few paces from where I stood. The first thought that flashed through my mind was, *Another raccoon?*

Except these eyes were different. More yellow. More piercing.

I pointed the light beam straight at it and discovered...a wolf?

I froze. For a nanosecond, I told myself it might be a coyote, but the idea crumbled because I know the difference. Coyotes are much smaller, lanky-looking, with tall, pointy ears and a narrow snout. This thing was big and broad, with rounded ears and a blocky snout.

It can't be, I thought. There were no wolves in Ohio. But here one was.

Moving slowly, I reached into my pocket for the gun. As I slid it out, I wondered: If this pocket pistol was big enough for a dog, but too small for a bear, what would it do to a wolf?

The creature stood there, glaring at me, and all of a sudden, the silence of the night felt wrong. I realized then that no fireflies were flashing.

Turning my attention back to the wolf, I said, "Scram." Although I said it on instinct, I immediately felt foolish. Isn't that what you'd say to a cat?

The wolf gave zero reaction.

Then, I noticed another pair of glowing eyes in the distance.

I pointed the light beam that way and spotted a second wolf, pacing at the opposite end of the clearing. For the first time, I felt scared, my heart beating as fast as a woodpecker hammering on a tree.

For a fleeting second, I thought about calling for help. The idea quickly deflated when I realized I had left my phone in the tent. But it wouldn't have done me much good anyway. Who would I call? How long would it take someone to find us? I was on my own here.

Checking to see if there might be other wolves, I slowly swept across the clearing with the flashlight, and when my beam fell on the tents...

Wait...what? My mind erupted in panic.

I blinked, trying to make sense of the sight.

A shadow crawled out through the entry flaps of the twins' tent, and I immediately knew it wasn't either of the boys.

Someone was in there?

I stood there in shock as the figure rose to a standing position, then turned back to face the tent. Black clothing, like a long robe with full-length sleeves, shrouded the intruder.

The twins came crawling out next. They tucked in on either side of the figure but didn't look my way. My brain screamed, *What's happening here? Is this some sort of sick prank?*

"Hey!" I yelled.

The only one who turned to face me was the person who had no business being there. They were too far away for me to make out any facial features in the darkness. I only saw a blank, pale face under a dark head covering. And the eyes. They seemed to glow, a sickly, jaundiced yellow.

What happened next took my breath away: The twins each took one of the figure's hands, and all three began walking off in the opposite direction.

I moved to release the gun's safety, but doing it while holding the flashlight with shaking hands was no simple task. I fumbled with it until I felt it snap into the unlocked position, then pointed the pistol at the wolf and said, "Back off, bitch!"

My threat had no effect. Instead, the wolf snarled and drew in.

I switched my eyes over near the tents.

They were heading toward...the pond?

"Stop!"

None of them reacted.

Without giving it a second thought, I aligned the gun's sights on the wolf and pulled the trigger. *Crack.*

The wolf remained standing without flinching. That's the problem with handguns: compared to rifles, they're hard to aim—especially tiny ones like this pocket pistol. I lined up the sights again, straining to hold my hands still as I pulled the trigger, slow and steady, as they taught me at the shooting range. *Crack.*

This time, the wolf recoiled and then dropped.

I launched into a sprint, chasing after them. It's not like I thought I could outrun the other wolf. I just knew it was too far to hit, and I couldn't let them get away.

By the time I passed the tents, they were at the pond's edge, cutting through the cattails, dropping as they descended the bank.

Yeah, they were going into the water. So, not only was this thing taking the twins, but it was planning to drown them.

And the weirdest part of all? My brothers were going along with it. Willingly. As if they were in a trance or something.

As I ran, a blur shot out of the darkness. I saw it flying at me, almost in slow motion. All I could do was duck, but I ducked so hard that I lost my balance and stumbled to the ground.

It was the second wolf, landing in a tumble a few feet from me, with a yelp. I had dropped the flashlight when I fell, but still had the gun. I scrambled to my knees and aimed as it righted itself and turned to face me, snarling.

Crack! The thing flipped backward and fell on its side. At point-blank range, I had hit it on the first shot, like straight out of an action movie.

I lunged for the flashlight beam glowing in the grass. Climbing to my feet, I steered the light at the pond, searching frantically for some sign of my brothers. All I saw was a dark gap in the water where the three of them had gone into the pond, leaving a part in the duckweed layer.

I rushed to the water's edge, where I dropped the flashlight and pistol onto the ground, knowing they'd be useless if they got wet. The knife in my pocket would be my weapon.

Fueled by adrenaline, I crashed down the bank, following the trail they'd trampled through the cattails, and dove into that black water. As I plunged below the surface, the sudden coolness made my skin prickle, and my mind filled with a mix of panic and terror. Although I had to save my brothers, the last place I wanted to be was this dank pond with God-knows-what lurking out of sight.

I swung my arms in long underwater strokes, grasping for them as I swam, but bumping into nothing.

Staying submerged as long as I could, my lungs were soon aching for air. I popped out, panting. When I wiped my eyes and looked around, I still saw no one. After taking a deep inhale, I dove back down, heading further into the pond.

Again, I felt nothing. With my lungs burning for oxygen, I resurfaced near the middle. A log floated on the surface in front of me. I hadn't noticed it before. Then, I spotted something climbing out of the pond opposite where we'd gone in. I blinked.

Three figures.

As they climbed out of the water, I treaded water, bewildered and struggling to catch my breath.

I questioned whether I might be dreaming. *No way,* I thought, considering the rush of sensations I was immersed in. The pond's fetid smell, the coolness of the water, the wet sounds my gasps made on the surface. It was all too *real.*

As I dove under the floating log to go after them, I realized something was amiss: the duckweed was gone. The entire surface was now clear.

When I resurfaced, I noticed not only was the duckweed gone, but a faint purple-colored mist hung above the pond. I resisted the urge to examine it and swam furiously to catch up.

Now, within a body length of the cattails, I felt for and found the bottom with my feet. I scrambled up the slope, but kept slipping on the mud. With water pouring off my body, I slogged through the last of the cattails and lurched onto dry ground, searching for them.

Moving shadows receded into the woods. Despite all my efforts, I was no closer. I staggered up the last stretch of the embankment and chased after them, my pace slowed by my waterlogged boots.

Inside the trees, the leaf cover blotted out the moonlight. Even though I could hardly see, I couldn't afford to slow down, so it wasn't long before I took a branch to the face. The twig poked me in the eye, making me see a burst of orange light. The brief shot of excruciating pain filled my entire head, as if I'd been impaled with a hot poker.

I held my eye with an open palm and stumbled onward at a more cautious pace. Up ahead, the three figures dropped from view when they descended into a gully. I pressed on, using my arm to shield my face from other unseen branches.

When I arrived at the edge of the gully, they were already at the bottom, downstream from a modest waterfall, little more than a summertime trickle. Just beneath where I stood, a wooden viewing platform had been attached to some trees.

The three figures meandered along the ravine at the bottom of the gully, which ended at a gravel roadway, off in the distance. Something on that road caught my eye. I squinted, studying it with one good eye and one throbbing one.

A black buggy?

That's when it hit me: the figure's long black skirt, full-length sleeves, black bonnet...what Amish women wear when they venture out.

Knowing I had no time to ponder this bizarre development, I turned my attention back to the terrain. A well-worn trail led to the platform. They had followed this path, but I had no clue what route they had taken beyond that point. Considering the steep drop-off below the platform, going down that way could be treacherous.

I decided that instead of following them down into the gully, I would continue along the ridge, hoping that this route would provide a steady descent to the roadway. If so, it would give me a shortcut.

At first, I tried to be quiet as I picked my way along the ridge, but that was slowing me down, so after stepping on and snapping a few twigs without anyone looking up, I quit worrying.

About the same time as they reached the roadway, I came to the end of the ridge and realized the mistake I'd made. I stood over a steep drop-off, with no simple path down the thirty-foot plunge. It was too late to go back, though. If I were going to have any shot at catching them, I had to find a way down, right there.

Feeling like I had no time to waste, I stepped off the edge, angling my heels to catch on the slope and, with any hope, slow my descent.

I give credit here to the gymnastics classes my mom made me suffer through until I turned sixteen. It may seem stupid, but I'm convinced that all that uneven bar practice prepared me for this moment. Because after I dropped a body length, I stopped myself by grabbing hold of a tree, exactly as my uneven bars training had taught me to do.

I shifted and aimed for another, catching it perfectly—my encore uneven bars move. I was one-third of the way down now, but the kidnapper and the twins were closing in on the buggy.

The next tree was off to the side, so reaching it would be a stretch. I dangled in that direction and pogoed off one foot to get there, catching the trunk with no more than an inch to spare.

But no sooner had I taken hold of it than the tree gave a cracking sound, and as my weight pulled against it, the damned thing snapped, sending me into a free fall. I landed on a thick trunk, right on the small of my back, grunting with a jolt of agony.

The idea of a broken back flashed through my mind, and I pictured myself lying there, paralyzed, while my brothers were taken away.

My God, could this nightmare get any worse?

That was the first time I consciously thought, *I should've listened to Mom.*

But the pain in my back told me I couldn't be paralyzed. I would have felt *nothing* if my spinal nerves had been severed.

Get going, I told myself. *You can do this.* I wasn't sure of that, though.

You must *do this. That* I couldn't argue with.

With a grunt, I unwrapped myself from the tree, which sent me sliding down the last body length of the slope. I tumbled into a heap in the ditch, about ten yards behind the carriage, and lay there for a second, assessing my injured back before convincing myself I could get up.

Pushing onto my hands and knees, I peeked through the weeds and caught a glimpse of the woman guiding the twins into the buggy.

As I rose to my feet, the soreness in my back shot down my legs. I told myself it was only a bruise, and I couldn't let it stop me. With a grimace, I straightened up.

The woman climbed in, and the carriage soon began moving. I heard the muffled clopping of the horse's hooves on the gravel roadway.

Fighting through my lower body aches, I climbed out of the ditch and stumbled after the buggy. At first, the distance between us shrank, and if I could have run at my usual speed, I'm sure I would have caught it. But with the pain in my back slowing me down, my run was more like a shuffle.

While I looked for something on the back of the carriage to latch onto, I realized it was picking up speed, and I was losing ground. I tried to run faster, but couldn't.

I vaguely noticed an old house and barn on one side of the road, half hidden by overgrowth. Both buildings were so dilapidated, they must have been abandoned decades ago. I recognized the distinct shape of the house: angular and symmetrical, a style that Dad had pointed out time and again on our trips through Amish country, the form of Old Order Amish homes.

As we passed the house, I could tell the horse was hitting its stride, and I was falling further behind. My heart sank with the realization that I could no longer reach it, even if I *could* run at full speed.

Although all hope of catching them had gone up in smoke, I had to keep after that buggy, to at least know where it was heading.

I trudged down the road as fast as my exhausted, battered body could carry me, watching those skinny wheels bounce over the gravel, listening to the sound of the horse's hooves grow quieter as it pulled away.

Chapter 4

When the buggy went around a bend, I lost sight of it. I tried picking up my pace more than ever, fearing that by the time the road straightened back out, I'd have fallen so far behind that it would be gone from view completely.

Relief washed over me when I rounded the corner, and the carriage reappeared. I also spotted the ruins of another abandoned house, built in the same simple Amish style as the last, and just as dilapidated.

Seeing that house prompted me to note my surroundings. We were in a valley with no signs of civilization. On either side of the road, the landscape alternated between woodland stretches and overgrown meadows, with only the two abandoned properties, and none of the land being actively farmed.

I tried to guess how far we'd gone down this country road. I figured I'd been chasing after the buggy for at least ten minutes, but with my bruised back hobbling me, I couldn't have gone more than a mile.

Up ahead, the carriage slowed to a crawl. Then, it turned into a driveway. At last, this was my chance to catch up.

I told myself to be smart. As much as I wanted to burst onto the scene and rescue my brothers, I couldn't be reckless. For all I knew, there might be others in the buggy, waiting to ambush me. Not to mention, they were moving onto private property, which meant I was trespassing, and in these parts, trespassers probably received the "shoot first, ask questions later" treatment. Maybe not the notoriously peaceful Amish, though. But who knows?

The carriage headed up the drive and disappeared behind the trees. I stepped into the ditch, edging along the tree line to stay hidden.

As I approached the driveway, I bumped into a rusty mailbox, causing a loose piece of sheet metal hanging underneath to squeak. I grabbed it and held it under the moonlight, examining the hand-painted words, worn thin with age:

BE STILL, AND KNOW THAT I AM GOD

I wasn't quite sure what that meant, but I had seen plenty of other biblical verse signs on mailboxes during our drive through Homer County. What gave me a shiver was how someone had scratched in a few extra characters, turning the word "God" into "Ungodly."

I looked at it twice to make sure I hadn't misread it. I hadn't. The extra letters were coated in rust. Something sharp—a nail, maybe—had been used to scratch through the paint, exposing the steel underneath, which had since oxidized. The person who did this had done it years ago.

Then, I noticed scratches across the first three words, so the sign had been changed to read:

KNOW THAT I AM UNGODLY

As unsettled as I felt seeing that, I couldn't dwell on it.

Letting go of the sign carefully so it wouldn't squeak, I pushed on, holding up behind the scrub of vegetation at the foot of the drive.

I peered up the dirt driveway and watched the carriage slowly ascend, as if the horse pulling it was laboring up the hill, like the one Mom kept us waiting behind on the way here. It was hard to believe that was just this morning. With the batshit stuff I was going through, it seemed like a year ago.

A narrow strip of woods lined the passage on either side. The buggy bounced over deep ruts, while tall weeds growing between the ruts brushed its underside. Ahead, at the top of the hill, a barn peeked through the trees, moonlight glistening off its slate roof.

Now that I knew where the kidnapper was taking my brothers, a thought popped into my head: should I go back to the camp and get my phone? If I brought it to where the driveway met the gravel road, its location service could tell the law where we were.

But what if there were no service in this valley? Then I thought about how even if I hurried, it would take me an hour to fetch the phone and return. No way could I leave my brothers alone for that long. I shoved the idea aside.

Gritting my teeth against my aching back, I crouched and followed the buggy, creeping up the ditch along one side of the driveway, ready to leap into the brush if anyone appeared.

As I made my way up the drive, a smaller building beside the barn came into view, and I noticed the smell of smoke.

When the carriage approached the top of the hill, I slowed to keep my distance. It turned at the end of the driveway and came to a stop in front of the barn.

A faint light blinked on from within the barn. Holding my breath, I backed slowly into the brush, ignoring the sting of thorns poking me as I pressed into hiding.

Somebody stepped out through the open barn door, carrying an oil lantern. The dim light cast eerie shadows over a sagging, wrinkled face, while a long gray beard, but no mustache, revealed it to be an Amish man. He moved like the old people in the assisted living center where my 88-year-old great-grandmother lives: unsteady and all hunched over.

Then, it hit me: he was wearing one of those straw hats that Amish men wear. *A hat at night?* But everything was strange here, so I let it go.

As he made his way toward the buggy, the light glinted on something he was carrying, and I soon realized it was a rifle. Or was it a shotgun? I was too far away to tell.

On instinct, I grabbed my knife from my shorts' pocket. It wouldn't do me much good from this distance if he spotted me, but it was all I had. I unfolded it and clasped my fingers around the handle.

The man stopped at the hitching post and placed the gun and lantern on the ground. He picked up a rope coiled on one end of the post, unspooled it as he walked over to the horse, and tied it off.

With one arm wrapped under the gun, he lifted the lantern and approached the buggy's side, his free hand extended. The woman's head poked out like a turtle's, then her shoulders. Neither of them spoke as he helped her down.

The light from the oil lamp gave me a better look at her clothing. Her dress, an apron, a cape over her shoulders, a bonnet covering her head, and her shoes were all the color of coal. She stepped to the side while the man returned to the buggy.

My stomach clenched when a straw hat emerged from the opening. Its smaller size told me what I didn't want to believe, but already knew. When the hat tilted up, my fears were confirmed. It was Xavier, wearing an Amish boy's hat. I could tell it was him because he had a slightly fuller face than Dustin.

When Xavier's upper body came out, he was wearing an Amish boy's shirt. I wondered how he could have allowed someone to dress him this way. I tried reading his expression, but it was too dark, and I was too far away.

Xavier took the man's hand and climbed down. Instead of the shorts he had been wearing, he was dressed in long, Amish-style pants, held up with suspenders. He was barefoot, though. That's when I noticed the man wasn't wearing shoes either. Xavier and the old man wandered over to the woman, and Xavier tucked in beside her.

When she wrapped her hand around his shoulder, I almost screamed. I wanted to run out, tackle her, grab her by the throat, and squeeze with all my might. It took everything in me to stand still and keep quiet, but I knew if I was going to save them, I couldn't just dash out into an open clearing. I needed to wait for my opportunity.

Dustin followed, wearing the same kind of outfit and barefoot, as well. He took a position on the woman's opposite side, and she draped her other arm around him.

The oil lamp shone enough light on the boys' faces to reveal something that gave me goosebumps: they both wore empty expressions, like they weren't all there.

The man headed back toward the barn, carrying the gun over his shoulder. When the woman turned to follow, steering the twins on either side of her, she began singing. The plain melody sounded monotone, almost like a chant. The old man soon joined her, and the bleak sound of it gave me chills.

I saw more movement near the barn. Two other figures stepped out, who turned out to be women, dressed exactly as the first, in long skirts with full-length sleeves, aprons, capes, and bonnets on their heads. The only difference was that their aprons and capes were white.

The white-aproned women waited as the couple and the boys passed, then stepped in, close behind. They too joined in the hymn, creating a horrible sound, each person a bit off-key from the others. I couldn't make out any words, but since it sounded a bit like German, I decided it must be Pennsylvania Dutch, the first language of the Amish.

Heading off in the opposite direction, the group sang as they walked, looking and sounding like some sort of twisted funeral procession. I could still recognize the shorter forms of my brothers, who had fallen in with the march.

The buggy soon blocked my view. I stepped out of the brush and tiptoed up the drive, holding the knife at the ready. When the six figures came back into sight, they were nearing the patch of woods behind the barn. A campfire glowed from a clearing in the trees, which I figured was the source of the smoky smell.

When I finally arrived at the top of the drive, the stretch of overgrowth transitioned into lawn, and a house appeared. The home had no power lines and, like the others I'd passed, was built in the telltale simple shape of an Amish house. *This* one wasn't dilapidated, though. Dim light from an oil lamp glowed within. The windows were open, as you'd expect on a hot summer night without air conditioning, but I saw no one.

As I scurried across the open yard, a dog, which must've been snoozing in the shadows of the home's front porch, lifted its head and looked my way. For a second, I thought he might bark, but instead, he started wagging his tail. He got up and hopped off the porch onto the grass, coming toward me. Even though I was thankful he looked friendly, I groaned to myself, knowing he could totally blow my cover.

I raced to the back of the carriage and hunkered down, waiting for the dog to arrive. He came in with his head lowered and his tail swinging, like I was his long-lost sister. He was a full-sized dog, old and mangy. Must've been a mutt, but he looked a bit like our dog Bluey, so he probably had some golden retriever mixed in.

"Sorry, buddy," I whispered as I gave him a few pets on his matted fur. "You need to leave me alone."

He licked my face. I quit petting him, hoping he'd get the message, but he dropped to his side and rolled over in the dirt, belly up.

The horse snorted from the front of the carriage, startling me so badly that I almost dropped the knife.

I peeked around the buggy and caught glimpses of shadows shifting between the tree trunks in the woods, backlit by the firelight. I waited long enough to confirm that two of the figures were shorter than the others.

Leaving the dog where he was, I snuck around the buggy's side, noticing the twins' clothes heaped on the floor. I hesitated, unsure whether to take them, but decided to leave them be. I needed my brothers. It didn't matter what they wore.

I scampered to the barn and slipped along its shadows to where it ended in front of the woods, waiting there to get a lay of the land and devise a plan. The dog righted himself and lazily wandered back to the porch.

The only other sign of movement was the figures in the woods, shifting around the firelight, while the only sound was the incessant drone of that awful hymn.

Between the blank looks on my brothers' faces and the way they were following this woman around, it seemed clear she had them under some kind of spell. But getting them away from her should break it, right?

As far as I could tell, the old man was the only one with a weapon. I had my knife. Was I ready to use it? You'd better believe it. I had no choice.

If I could get close, I could catch the man off guard, stab him, and take his gun. He was old and frail-looking, so even with my bruised back, it wouldn't take much to overpower him, especially with the element of surprise working in my favor.

Once I had the gun, I could threaten the women with it. Or shoot them, if that's what it took to save my brothers. Before he got ALS, Dad had taught me how to work a .22 rifle.

But if his gun turned out to be a shotgun, would I know how to use it? I had never handled one. Was there that much difference? Pfft. Maybe not, but in the dark, when I was in a hurry, the slightest difference could seriously trip me up.

I tried to figure out how best to sneak up on them. If I followed their path, they'd be more likely to see me coming. It would make more sense to approach from a different direction. Maybe I could enter the woods from the open area behind the house, but I needed a better look.

I crept across the short stretch of grass to the smaller building, and when I brushed against it, chickens clucked softly from inside. I froze, but the creepy-sounding hymn continued from the woods.

Apparently, this small building was a henhouse. I had to be careful not to rile up the hens, which would *definitely* give me away.

I tiptoed to the opposite end of the coop, the side facing the home. The patch of woods ended there, and beyond it, there was a garden behind the house, with sweet corn at the back, grapevines at the front, and neat vegetable rows in between.

I scooted across the clearing and into the garden, ducking into the grapevines and pausing there to catch my breath.

Although the eye I had poked was still tender, I had no problems seeing with it. Maybe it was because I was so amped up by what I was doing, but my back didn't feel as sore as it had. My forearm was cramping from how tightly I gripped the knife, though. I switched it to the other hand and opened and closed my fingers to relieve the tension while watching what I could see of the procession, still circling the fire. The two shorter figures were still visible.

As much as I couldn't stand the sound of that horrible chanting, I was glad they were still carrying on, since it would help cover any noise from my approach.

But then I went stiff. I cocked my head and listened carefully. I almost convinced myself I had misheard, but my blood ran cold when I realized I hadn't.

The boys—*my brothers*—were singing, too.

Chapter 5

Telling myself I couldn't worry about *why* my brothers were chanting, or *how* they'd suddenly learned another language, I peeked out from the grapevines and watched the procession circling the fire. The boys remained glued to either side of that woman.

I decided to sneak into the woods from the back end of the garden, so I hunched low and headed that way, following the furrows between the produce plants.

Squeezing between the cornrows, I watched through a little gap as they circled the fire, singing their eerie hymn. There was a narrow stretch of grass I would need to cross, but once I reached the woods, if I kept low, the brush would keep me hidden.

Figuring my back would tolerate it, I decided to army crawl. I dropped to the ground, gulped in a big breath, and pushed out from the cover of the cornstalks with the knife in one hand.

Since I was fully exposed, I crossed the short expanse of grass quickly. I wasted no time pushing into the tall weeds growing at the edge of the woods, clenching my teeth as twigs and thorns tore up my bare legs and arms.

I moved slowly to avoid snapping branches. A mosquito buzzed in my ear, but keeping still and silent meant I had to ignore it.

The weeds thinned out after a short stretch, but since the firelight didn't reach this far and the tree canopy above me blocked the moonlight, I convinced myself I was still hidden in the darkness and continued edging closer, at a snail's pace.

By this point, I had a better view of the clearing, with the fire at its center. About the size of our two-car garage, the clearing left a gap in the tree cover, allowing moonlight to shine through while the smoke and embers swirled out.

As the procession circled the fire, I caught glimpses of each of their faces. First, I saw the man. He looked even older than his posture suggested, with furrows on his cheeks and forehead deeper than the driveway ruts.

When my brothers came around, I studied their faces. Their mouths moved as they sang along in the dreadful hymn, but they both still wore the same blank expression. A trance is what I had called it, and the term seemed to fit. As they rounded the circle, shadows spread across their faces until I lost sight of them.

The two white-aproned women followed. The first looked about eighteen, like me. Her face was pretty, but she wore the same blank expression as my brothers. When I turned my gaze to the second, my breath caught. She was a carbon copy of the first. *They* were identical twins, too. This *couldn't* be a coincidence.

They passed, and when the circle looped back around, I got my first good look at the black-aproned woman between my brothers.

At first, I thought it was a trick of the firelight, but as I held my stare, an unmistakable, hideous image came into focus. Although she appeared to be a young woman, her eyes were milky yellow. I immediately thought of my grandma's elderly dog, whose cataracts were so bad that he was practically blind. This woman's eyes were like his, *but yellow.*

My mind reeled. What was I facing here?

At that moment, I began kicking myself for not going back to get my phone. I was in *so* far over my head.

The old man stepped out of the circle on the other side of the fire and began feeding it with branches from a stack. Although I remained beyond the reach of the light, it would expand as the flames grew. Knowing I risked being seen if I got any closer, I stopped moving.

I leaned back on my heels and examined the area surrounding the fire. It was neatly tended, with the ground trampled smooth and cleared of debris. This couldn't have been the first time the site had been used this way.

After the man finished stoking the fire, he didn't rejoin the moving procession. Instead, he stood at the edge of the clearing, opposite me and on the other side of the fire, with both hands gripping his gun, at the ready.

I cursed my bad luck. If he had been standing with his back to me, I could have jumped him, stabbing him in the back. I told myself to keep waiting and prayed my chance would come.

When the twin women passed the man, they left the procession and took positions beside him. Firelight danced on their pretty faces, but their eyes remained vacant and distant.

The chanting grew louder, and the woman with the yellow eyes tilted her face upward. Without looking where she was stepping, she slowly led my brothers around the fire three more laps. Then she stopped, with her back toward me, steering them beside her.

The hymn ended abruptly, and an unsettling silence took its place. The fire crackled, and a breeze rustled the leaves above. I held my breath, straining to keep still to avoid making noise.

The yellow-eyed woman removed her hands from the boys and reached into a pocket on one side of her apron. She removed a small pouch and began reciting in Pennsylvania Dutch. She poured the pouch's contents into her open hand, closed it with a fist, and raised it over the fire. Her voice rose in volume. When she turned her hand over and opened it, dumping the contents over the fire, a thick column of purple smoke rose into the air.

Seconds later, something hit the ground at the edge of the clearing, and I flinched. Then another smacked nearby. Soon, the entire ground within the clearing was being pelted from the sky.

It wasn't long before a few punched through the tree cover and bounced my way. I turned my eyes and stared at one, then another. They were white and round. For a second, I thought they were golf balls, but that made no sense. A moment later, my brain connected the dots...

We were in a *hailstorm.*

Ever so slowly, I tilted my head back and looked up at the sky above the clearing. A thick cloud, churning in a vortex, unleashed this barrage of hail. Shredded leaves began drifting down from the branches above me, and several hailstones shot through, unobstructed. If this continued, it wouldn't be long before all the leaf cover protecting me would be stripped from the branches.

Hail bounced off the people around the fire, but none of them reacted. Then it dawned on me why they were wearing hats and bonnets: they'd been *expecting* this.

The hail stopped as suddenly as it had begun, and the scene fell silent. The cloud that had formed out of nowhere thinned, allowing the moonlight to filter back through.

All around me, hailstones littered the ground, nearly blanketing it. Steam rose from the fire, which had been knocked back, but was still burning. The man went to work rearranging the half-burned branches and adding more from the stack.

The woman guided my brothers down onto their knees. Once they were settled, she walked around the fire. The old man stepped away as she approached the twin women. She steered them to their knees, side by side, like the boys, while speaking in a commanding tone, using words I couldn't understand.

The man bent over to pick something up from the ground—a glass pitcher. The yellow-eyed woman took it from him, turned to the first twin woman, and spoke to her. The twin woman nodded and voiced a single word, then tilted her head back, allowing the yellow-eyed woman to pour liquid from the pitcher over her forehead.

After the yellow-eyed woman repeated this sequence with the second twin woman, she handed the pitcher back to the man.

With her back toward me, she blocked my view of what came next. All I could tell was that, using both hands, she did something to the first twin woman, then the second. Next, she spun around to face the fire, with an object held in each hand.

I gasped when I realized one hand held a knife, covered in blood.

She raised the other hand over the fire, but I still couldn't make out what she was grasping.

When I looked back at the twin women, I had to stifle a scream. Their mouths hung open, with blood dripping down their chins. A wave of horror rushed through my mind as I realized what she'd done.

The evil woman had cut out their tongues.

I kept thinking, *I'm not seeing this.* But with plenty of moonlight and firelight, there was no denying that I was.

Somehow, those poor women stayed kneeling, with those blank expressions still plastered on their faces.

My brothers remained kneeling with their backs toward me. She hadn't cut their tongues out, but they might be next.

I felt my whole body shaking. Part of me wanted to flee. Another part of me wanted to run to my brothers. But some small rational voice in my mind told me both choices would be foolish.

In truth, fear might've paralyzed me. Whatever it was, I stayed put, tense and motionless, cowering in the darkness.

Mom was right, I thought, fighting back tears. *I never should have done this on my own.* If only we had skipped this backpacking idea...we'd be home, sleeping safely in our beds.

I vowed then that if I could get us out of here, this would be the last time I ever went backpacking.

Before I yanked myself out of my spiral into self-pity, I reflected on how, when I hurt my back falling down that slope, I had wondered if things could have gotten any worse. They sure had.

The deranged woman slipped the knife into her apron pocket, then took one tongue in each hand. She circled the fire to where my brothers were kneeling and stopped before them. For a panic-stricken moment, I thought she might do the same thing to them. The only thing keeping me sane was knowing she'd put the knife away.

With my heart galloping, I waited to see what she'd do next, readying myself to launch out of the darkness if I saw she was about to hurt them.

She spoke again, simultaneously holding one tongue before each of my brothers' faces. They were facing away, so I couldn't be sure, but they appeared to...*lick them.* I pressed a fist against my mouth to stifle a gag.

She stepped back until she stood halfway between my brothers and the twin women, angling herself so I could see her profile in the rekindled firelight.

With one hand raised in the air, the tongue dangling from her fingertips, she tilted her head back and closed her eyes, winking out their sickly yellow glimmer. Her mouth fell open, exposing the most vile-looking pointed teeth. Her own tongue extended out, pausing to lick the air like a snake, before unfurling even further.

As that foul tongue stretched even further, the creature's lower jaw hinged down impossibly far, until her chin bumped against her neck. Her tongue kept on growing to a freakish length, reaching all the way out to her raised hand.

Her outstretched tongue flicked at, then wrapped around the severed tongue, before withdrawing, retracting into her gaping mouth with the tongue in tow.

She closed her mouth, tilted her head forward, opened her milky yellow eyes, and began chewing. I heard the meat crunch and tear as those sharp teeth shredded it. Blood glistened on her lower lip and dribbled down her chin.

My head swam with a suffocating sensation, like I was on the verge of passing out. I told myself to breathe.

We weren't just dealing with a kidnapper. This was...something satanic. The modified word on the sign underneath the mailbox flashed in my mind: *ungodly.*

I almost threw caution to the wind and charged this monster with my knife, but I fought the urge, warning myself how futile this would be. God only knew what this thing was capable of.

I tore my gaze away and looked at the others. The man was only half watching, looking almost bored. The white-aproned twins stared blankly ahead with open, bloody mouths. My brothers didn't move.

The entity licked its lips and then went for the other tongue, repeating the gruesome routine that had played out with the first.

Her chin bounced as she chomped, then she gulped it down like a hungry dog.

Next, she circled the fire, then stopped behind the twin women. She began speaking again. One at a time, she reached under their chins, pushed their mouths closed, and pulled them onto their feet.

She led the pair around the fire, circling it three times, then stopped in front of my brothers. Lifting one woman's hand, she placed it on the top of Dustin's head, then did the same to Xavier's head with the other woman's hand. She stepped aside but continued speaking, her voice rising into a wail.

With blood coating their lips and chins, the women tilted their heads back and faced the sky. Unable to breathe, I watched as the entire scene stood still for what seemed like forever.

It's hard to explain what happened next. Suddenly, in a blink, the women were sucked backward into the flames.

The wicked thing went silent.

My jaw hung open as I tried to process what I'd witnessed. I was on the verge of deciding my brothers would be next when I noticed a shimmer of movement...two vague shadows shifting on the other side of the fire, low to the ground. I squinted, and before long, I recognized the shadows.

Wolves.

The twin women had been turned into wolves.

The animals circled one another at the man's feet, turning their heads almost frantically, like trying to get their bearings on new-found surroundings.

One wolf stopped abruptly and looked my way, its eyes glowing in the firelight, its ears perking forward. I shrank back as the creature bared its teeth and wrinkled its snout. The other wolf picked up on the signal and turned toward me. A split second later, its eyes lit up, and its ears rose; it, too, began snarling.

The woman whipped around to face me. Her cloudy yellow eyes homed in on me instantly, as though even through those cataracts, she had highly sensitive night vision. She pointed and shouted in her language.

The wolves split apart, each circling in opposite directions around the fire, coming at me from either side, in a pack hunt mentality. I rose to my knees, clutching the knife, preparing to plunge it into the first one that leaped.

The yellow-eyed being yelled something else, and the wolves halted, beyond my reach. One of them rounded behind me, so I turned away from the fire in that direction.

By the time I heard a twig snap behind me, it was too late.

CHAPTER 6

I WOKE UP FACE-DOWN on a filthy wooden floor, with the sound of flies buzzing all around me.

Although I had zero recollection of what had happened and no sense of where I was, I knew everything was wrong. My head ached so fiercely that I could hardly think. I couldn't lift it, either. It felt as heavy as a boulder.

When I tried opening my eyes, the brightness of the light doubled the pain.

I moaned and shifted, grinding dirt into my sweaty cheek. Wherever I was, it was hot, the air stuffy.

I realized flies were crawling around on the back of my head. When I raised my hand there, I winced, feeling what I immediately knew was dried blood, clotted in my hair. The back of my head was so swollen it didn't feel real.

Then, I felt a twinge in my bruised back, and the horrible turn of nighttime events came back to me. The kidnapping. The ritual at the fire in the woods. The hailstorm. The wolves. And maybe the worst of the nightmare, the tongues. The word *ungodly* flashed in my mind, and I shuddered. Where were my brothers? Hell...where was *I?*

I strained to push open my eyelids. My vision blurred. I rubbed my eyes and tried again, fighting through the throbbing sensation racking my head.

The flies took flight, and I heard the sound of birds chirping, which made me realize the blindingly bright light was sunlight.

I rolled onto my side, and something clanked on the floor beside my hip. A weird, faint sound followed, then died off. It seemed familiar, but I couldn't place it.

Trying to focus my eyes on my surroundings, I could see I was in a tiny room with unpainted wooden walls. Sunbeams streamed in through a small, grimy windowpane near the top of the wall, spotlighting a swirl of dust filling the air.

I tilted forward to get a look at the adjoining wall, which was centered with a heavy wooden door.

When I rolled over to examine the other side, I heard that clanking noise again, as well as the other strange sound.

I suddenly became aware of something clenched around my waist. Groping it, I felt leather. It seemed like a thick belt, riding above my hips. I followed it and came across a gap, exposing a section of steel. On my opposite side, the same thing. Tiny steel hinges.

I'd been shackled.

Panicking, I yanked on the belt. It didn't budge, though. I reached around and discovered a loop at the small of my back. A chain was secured to the loop with a bulky padlock. I realized then that the chain clanking was one of those sounds I'd been hearing, but couldn't place.

It took a major effort, but I managed to sit up. The room spun, and my head felt like it was being squeezed in a massive vise. I pressed my open palms over my eyes and took shallow breaths, praying for the painful head rush to subside.

When I felt ready, I blinked my eyes open and looked around. The other end of the chain was looped through a U-bolt attached to a floor plank. I gave it a good tug, which accomplished nothing other than proving the chain was solidly anchored.

The racket I made stirred up that other noise, but my brain was still too gummed up to identify it.

I turned to examine the other parts of the tiny room. A flimsy door took up one corner. Behind me, just beyond my reach, sat a stack of burlap bags. I studied the words printed on the top bag: *POULTRY FEED.*

In my haze, I couldn't remember what poultry meant at first, but then it hit me, and I realized what that other sound had been. I slapped the floor, and sure enough, chickens clucked from the other side of the wall.

I was in a chicken coop. In a little vestibule, to be exact, separated from where the hens were kept.

Something fluttered above me, and I flinched, only to discover it was a moth crossing the room. It settled on the windowpane.

In the last remaining corner sat an old galvanized bucket. Beside it, a clear glass pitcher, much like one Mom displayed in our kitchen. Mom called it "depression glass." It had been Grandma's. Or maybe it was my great-grandmother's. Mom had told me whose it was, but now, I couldn't remember. Thinking of them all made my heart ache and drove home how much I wished I were with them. I would've settled for anywhere but where I was.

The pitcher appeared to be filled with water, which got me licking my lips. They were rough and dry, and so was my tongue. Was I dehydrated? As far as I knew, the last time I peed was when I had left my tent. Right before this nightmare began. How long ago was that? It seemed so distant.

Anyway, I still didn't need to go. No, that wasn't quite right. I probably *could* have gone if I tried, but with no toilet, I had no problem holding it. Either way, yeah, I *must* be dehydrated. But I didn't dare drink from that pitcher.

Although I knew it would be a struggle, I had to look out that little window. I rolled onto my knees, paused to collect myself, then climbed to my feet, the chain clattering as I rose. Everything swayed, so I leaned against the wall to steady myself, feeling like I was going to throw up.

I examined the room. It was a little wider than I was tall, but three times longer from front to back. Above me were open rafters under a corrugated tin roof, sloping down from the back toward the front. There was an opening along the top of either end, lined with chicken wire. For airflow, I guess.

The U-bolt sticking out of the floor where my chain was attached was closer to the back, so I could easily reach the bucket and the water pitcher. It didn't look like I'd be able to reach the heavy entrance door or the flimsy door into the coop, though. I felt too unsteady to try just yet.

Instead, I stepped up to the window, dragging the chain along the wooden slats. A feather lay on the windowsill. I picked it up and examined it. It had varying colors of brown and was long, like a tail feather. I brushed it over the back of my hand, feeling the smooth sensation, then tucked the pointy quill into a crevice between the siding boards near the window.

The window opening was the size of a shoebox. Even if I weren't tethered to the floor, there was no way I'd be able to squeeze through the frame.

The moth was still in the middle of the windowpane, where it had landed earlier. I brushed it aside carefully, and it resettled in the corner of the glass.

Sunlight shone on my face, straining my eyes. Shielding the glare with one hand, I stood on my tiptoes and leaned forward to look out.

The glass was so smudged I could hardly see through it. I used the meaty part of my fist to try to wipe it, cutting through a jungle of spiderwebs. My attempt to clean the window made little difference because the outside was even dirtier, and there was nothing I could do to clean that.

I gazed through the cloudy glass, trying to make out the view. After a while, I realized it wasn't just dirt on the pane; my vision was blurring. I strained to focus.

The sky was blue and cloudless, and the sun sat low, barely peeking over the distant trees, telling me it was still early. Unless it was late in the day—but I couldn't imagine that.

The same house I had seen at night sat at the opposite end of a patch of lawn. Clothing fluttered on a clothesline strung across the front porch.

Movement behind the house caught my eye. Something in the garden. A straw hat. No, two of them. Two Amish boys, based on their clothing and small sizes.

They were dressed as my brothers had been when they came out of the buggy. Of course, this meant nothing, since Amish boys *all* dressed like that.

At the end of the garden stood the woman. I winced at the sight of her. *Ungodly* echoed in my brain.

She was no longer dressed in black. Instead, she wore a long, dark blue dress with a white head covering they call a kapp. The garb that

Amish women wear around the house. She was gesturing as if giving them orders.

I turned my gaze back to the boys, who were kneeling between the rows, either weeding or picking produce. They had bare feet, like the night before. Was that my brothers? I couldn't tell for sure. I wanted to believe it was, because that would mean they were okay. Well, maybe I couldn't say they were *okay,* but I *could* say they were alive. That was *something.*

I fought off the urge to pound on the window and yell, knowing nothing good would come from that, for them, or me.

When my calves started to burn from standing on my tiptoes, I turned around and leaned my back against the wall, wiping my sweaty brow on my shirt. I felt lightheaded and sick to the stomach.

Concussion, I thought as I prodded the giant knot on the back of my head. *That's right: concussions can make you nauseous.* That would explain my slow thinking, too. I had gotten a concussion in gymnastics a few years back, so I knew a little something about them.

Just then, the door rattled, startling me. I pulled myself upright and looked around for a weapon. My knife...where was it? I felt the pockets of my shorts, but they were empty. I stepped over to where the chain was tethered to the floor and grabbed a slack section of the chain, grasping it in both hands. It wasn't much, but it was all I had.

The deadbolt turned, and the knob rotated. The sound got the chickens clucking. *Bawwwk...bawk bawk bawk...bawwwk,* they seemed to be chanting.

I clenched my jaw and squeezed the chain as the door began swinging open.

A straw Amishman's hat appeared. But with his head tilted down, the hat's brim hid his face. A long gray beard hung down over his filthy shirt, with giant wet patches under his arms.

I braced myself as he lifted his head, waiting for the hat brim to clear his face, fully expecting something monstrous. To my surprise and relief, he appeared completely human—just old.

I don't think I've ever seen such a wrinkled face. His eyelids drooped and sagged, the same way my great-grandmother's eyelids did. His mouth hung open. A few of his teeth were missing, and the ones he still had were brown. He had to be at least ninety years old.

Was it the same son of a bitch who had clubbed me? Probably. If I had to guess, it was he who had locked me up in here, too.

I wanted to lunge at him, but I pictured a mad dog launching at an intruder, its leash snapping it back violently. I might have done it anyway if my head hadn't felt like a railroad spike had been sunk into it.

I could spit on him, I thought, but I told myself not to, knowing this would accomplish nothing.

He looked me over as if I were some sideshow curiosity. Thinking back on it now, I probably could've passed for a bulging-eyed, rabid creature who would have choked him with the chains if I weren't restrained.

The old man was holding a plate. He looked at me for a moment, squatted down, placed it on the floor, and then slid it toward me. Scrambled eggs, buttered bread, and two strips of bacon. Was this some sort of peace offering?

Or was it poisoned? Probably not, seeing as he could kill me in so many easier ways.

He grunted as he stood, like straightening up was no simple task. Once he was standing, he wobbled, then steadied himself. Watching how much he struggled to move, I decided he might be over ninety years old.

"You'll be able to reach that," he said, gesturing to the plate.

The flies homed in on the food in no time.

A dog appeared at his side. It was the same friendly mutt that had licked my face the night prior. He looked even mangier in the daylight.

The man shooed the dog. "Go on, Sonny. Git." His voice had that elderly, strained sound.

Sonny slunk off with his tail between his legs.

The old man turned back to me. "That pitcher..." He pointed at the depression glass pitcher behind me. "That's your drinking water. That bucket...that's your outhouse."

I stared at the bucket, trying to figure out what he was talking about. If a roll of toilet paper had been sitting beside it, I might have understood right away. But there was no toilet paper in sight, so it took my sluggish brain a minute to catch on. At the same moment it clicked, the door slammed shut.

"Hey!" I yelled in a croaking voice. "Hold on!"

The lock rattled.

"Please!"

The deadbolt clicked.

I thought about calling again, louder, but didn't bother. My head hurt too badly to yell, and anyway, it wasn't like he hadn't heard me. I stepped over to the window and pushed onto my tiptoes, watching him hobble off to the house.

He stopped at the side of the porch and reached over to a bundle that I couldn't make out, between my blurred vision and the dirty glass. It took me a while to realize he was petting Sonny.

He labored up the steps and pulled open the screen door, which slammed behind him when he disappeared into the house.

I pressed my forehead against the wooden windowsill, feeling my throat tighten. I took a deep breath and fought back the tears, knowing crying would do me no good.

My back itched, reminding me of the mosquitoes that had been feeding on me in the woods. I couldn't reach the itchy spots, so I turned around and leaned backward, using the wooden slats of the wall to scratch myself, as a bear would do.

My gaze drifted over to the plate of food. *There's no way I'm eating that,* I said to myself, waving off the flies hovering around my head.

I looked back at the pitcher of water sitting beside the bucket. *Or drinking that water. Or using that bucket as a toilet.*

Before the sun set on that first day, I'd be wrong on all three counts.

Chapter 7

My leash—that's what I started thinking of the chain as—was too short for me to reach either of the doors. This was by design, I'm sure. I found that if I got on my hands and knees and pulled the chain taut, I could just reach the plate. Although I had no plans to eat the food, it was good to know I had the option if I changed my mind. I imagined the cruelty of placing it beyond my reach.

I left the food for the flies and tugged on the leash a few times, as if my brain couldn't come to grips with me being trapped.

Giving up, I returned to the window to watch the boys in the garden. The ungodly woman wandered up, stood over them, and said something. They picked up their baskets and followed her into the back of the house.

Although the hazy pane never provided me with a clear view, the way they walked clinched it. That was *definitely* them.

Knowing my brothers were alive, I relaxed slightly. Hell, maybe I was in a more dire situation than they were now.

There was little chance they could see me peeking through that small, smudgy window. But if they could, I wondered if they would recognize me. Not if they were still in a trance.

Who else was around? I played back the memory of the fireside ritual. Aside from my brothers, it was just the old man and the tongue-eating woman. The twin women had turned into wolves. Where had they gone?

I dragged my leash over to the water pitcher, crouched down, and looked it over. The pitcher looked clean, the water clear. Putting my face near it, I took a sniff. It had that metallic, well-water odor, but it wasn't foul or anything.

I considered taking a drink, but decided against it. *Maybe later,* I thought. ...*if you get desperate enough.*

I poured some water over my free hand, using the bucket as a catch basin. After switching hands, I rinsed the other, then wiped some over my face. The coolness felt good.

I was about to dump some over my head wound when I remembered what Dad taught me on our backpacking trip after I sliced a finger while whittling with my jackknife: Never pour non-potable water over an open cut. I couldn't be sure that this water was clean.

Since I had nothing to dry off with except my grimy shirt, I let my face and hands air dry instead.

I forgot about my concussion and stood too quickly, triggering a woozy spell. I crumpled onto the stack of chicken feed bags and waited for my head to clear.

Think, I told myself. *You need a plan.*

It was a chore to keep focused, though, so no plan came to me.

The flies were relentless. I tried swatting them, but that did little good. Dad used to clap above the surface they were crawling on. The idea is that by the time your hands slap together, they'll take flight, and you can smash them in midair. I tried this with flies that landed on my legs, but it was hopeless. The concussion made it seem like I was moving in molasses.

I thought about my cell phone, sitting uselessly in the tent, its battery draining. It was now clear what a huge mistake I'd made not going back for it.

At some point, Mom would wonder why she hadn't heard from me. She'd text, but I wouldn't respond. I had shared my location, so she would know where my phone was. But what if the battery died? Would the location still show? Yeah, probably the last location would.

Plus, I had written out our itinerary. Then again, how long would it take her to start worrying?

Worse yet, even if she or the sheriff found the phone, how would they find *us?* I'd guess we were a mile and a half from where we'd camped. We might as well be in the next county.

What about bloodhounds? Hmm. Yeah, maybe. But wait...wouldn't the pond mess that up?

Shit, I thought. Hoping Mom would save us was no plan. I had to come up with something else.

I pushed up from the chicken feed sacks and dragged the chain over to where it was secured to the floor. From my knees, I jerked on it, as if I hadn't pulled hard enough before. It didn't budge, though. I stood, pulled the chain taut, and gave it the strongest yank I could summon. There was no hint of its yielding.

Feeling a wave of dizziness from the effort, I returned to my seat on the feed bags.

I looked over the scrapes and tears on my knees from crawling through the woods in shorts. Luckily, those wounds were nothing like the gash on the back of my head.

A dark spot on the side of my calf caught my attention. I stared at it, thinking at first it was a piece of dirt. But when I tried to flick it off, it stayed right there. It seemed like a fleck of dried leaf, with ragged edges, attached to my skin. When I leaned forward for a closer look, I had to stifle a screech.

A tick.

Attached to me, exactly as you'd expect in this never-ending nightmare.

The tick itself didn't bother me half as much as it would have the day prior. But seeing the demonic woman had given me a whole new perspective on what qualifies as vile. Compared to her, ticks were child's play—just nasty little blood-sucking insects.

What freaked me out was the diseases they carried, including Lyme disease, at the top of Mom's most-dreaded list. And there were others as well, such as Rocky Mountain spotted fever.

I held back the urge to tear the tick off, remembering how Dad had gotten one on his chest during our hike. He made me watch as he removed it. "Pull straight out, and never twist it," he said. "If you twist it, you might tear off its head. Then you'll have a tick head stuck in your body." I groaned.

He'd used tweezers, which of course I didn't have. I examined my fingernails, telling myself they'd work just as well.

As I pinched the tick's body between the tips of my fingernails, its tiny legs began wiggling. "Stay calm," I said out loud to myself, pulling slowly, stretching my skin up into a pointy tent. I wanted to yank the bastard out, but I knew with it anchored firmly inside me, steady tension was the way to go.

Pop. It suddenly released.

As soon as it came free, I wanted to fling it. But I resisted.

Its legs writhed in a frenzy. I examined it to confirm its head hadn't been left behind in my body, then squeezed my fingernails together until I felt a crunch. Its legs clenched and went still.

As soon as I flicked the thing away, I regretted not examining the pattern on its back first. I remember Dad telling me how a certain type carries Lyme disease.

For a moment, I wondered if I might be able to find it, but when I looked in the filthy area where I had ditched it, I knew there was zero chance of that. Plus, without my phone, I couldn't identify what species of tick it was, or which diseases that species carried, so I gave up on the idea.

I inspected the rest of my body but, thankfully, found no more ticks.

Above me, something creaked. I looked up at the open rafters, covered with a sheet of corrugated steel. It sounded again, the metal expanding as the warming sun rose in the sky.

This got me thinking. I stood and reached up, but the rafters were too high to touch, so I climbed onto the pile of feed bags and tried again. This time, I could reach. I pressed my fingertips against the steel, which was warm but not too hot to touch. I tested it in a few places. Although it flexed a little, it was screwed firmly to the rafters. And without being able to peel up the metal, the gaps at either end were far too narrow to climb through.

A wave of lightheadedness prompted me to sit back down.

As much as I tried to concentrate on cooking up an escape plan, my mind kept wandering. At one point, I found myself fidgeting with the red silicone ALS bracelet I was still wearing, which got me thinking about my best friend, Caryn Davis. I missed her so much I felt like crying.

The bracelet came from an ALS fundraiser that Caryn and her swim-team captain boyfriend, Herb, had organized through our school. Maybe it was all dumb luck, but they couldn't have planned it any better.

Our Cleveland Heights High School had a particularly famous alum: Travis Kelce, the football player. Yeah, that guy—Taylor Swift's fiancée. He actually went to our school. It felt surreal thinking about the normal, sane world out there, so far from my reach. I had always thought our famous alum was the coolest thing ever, but locked up in that chicken coop, I couldn't care less.

Anyway, after Travis and his brother, Jason, heard about the fundraiser, they promoted it on their *New Heights* podcast. Well, *yeah,* the fundraiser went viral, raising almost half a million dollars. To top it all off, Taylor Swift matched the amount raised, doubling the total.

A million bucks. Hard to believe.

Maybe money can help save lives, but not mine...or my brothers'.

Would I ever see Caryn again?

And what would Caryn think if she could see me now? She would never believe what deep shit I'd gotten myself into, that's for sure.

I thought about the hell I was living through. What a difference a few hours can make. Last night, everything happened so fast that I could barely keep up with it. Now, I was imprisoned in squalor, alone with my thoughts in this godforsaken henhouse, with *nothing* happening.

A bead of sweat ran down my temple. I wiped off my face using my shirt. It was *definitely* getting warmer.

All of a sudden, I felt a raging thirst. I looked over at the glass pitcher and thought about how I hadn't had to use the bathroom since I left the tent, and since I didn't exactly have to now, that wasn't a good sign.

As if it were piling on, my stomach growled. I turned to the plate of food, now covered with half a dozen flies, and swallowed away the gagging sensation I felt coming on.

Our bodies can skip meals, no problem, Dad had told me on our hike. *But don't screw around with dehydration.*

I looked back at the water. My shoulders slumped, and I nodded. "Okay," I said out loud before pushing up and heading that way.

Chapter 8

THE WATER FELT SO good going down, I went from sipping it to guzzling it in no time. I only stopped to burp, and when I looked at how much I'd drunk, I saw the pitcher was already half empty. I told myself not to overdo it, but I didn't listen.

It was the bang of the home's screen door that got me to stop. I put the pitcher down and pushed to my feet, straining to steady myself in the spinning room.

As the lock began rattling, I prepared for a fight. The door swung out to reveal the old man again. My vision blurred, so I couldn't tell what he was holding at first, but when my eyesight cleared, I realized it was the rifle.

"I need to feed the hens," he said, waving the flies away from the old plate of food, before reaching in and moving it outside.

I waited for him to say something else. Since he just stood there, I asked, "So?"

He put his free hand on his hip with his elbow jutting out, then furrowed his brow. "I didn't think this through all that well."

"Okay," I said, unsure of what he was expecting.

Although his Adam's apple was hidden behind his beard, I could tell it was bobbing back there. "Can you slide one of those feed bags over here?"

I looked at the stack of feed bags, then back at him. I narrowed my eyes and thought, *Maybe he's afraid of me.* The truth was, I probably could've kicked his ass if I didn't have concussion-head. *And if he didn't have that gun,* I added. Having said that, while I'm no rifle expert, what he was holding looked like an antique. Maybe it had been a World War I firearm.

But here he was, asking me to do him a favor. Maybe this was my chance to get some answers. "Where are my brothers?"

He rubbed his gray, scraggly beard and looked in the direction of the house, but said nothing.

I peeked out the window, searching for some sign of them, but saw no one.

"Why did you take them?"

The old man kept on scratching his long beard as he considered this. Eventually, he said, "*They* took them."

The word "they" caught me off guard. I had to stop and think about it. I was sure the gender-neutral pronoun thing hadn't caught on with the Amish. Did that mean others were working with the ungodly woman-thing? I decided not to dwell on it. I needed to focus on my brothers. "What are you going to do with them?"

He was still staring at the house, still rubbing his beard, but he gave no reply.

"What are you going to do with me?"

He turned back to give me an empty look, as though he had no clue, and said, "They'll decide."

For a minute, I wondered if he meant my brothers would decide. I realize now how stupid that sounds, but my mind wasn't working right. "Who is 'they?'" I asked, feeling like the conversation was turning into a variation of the Abbott and Costello comedy sketch

"Who's on First?" which Grandpa had shown me. I almost laughed, but it was more out of frustration than humor.

He cleared his throat like he was going to answer, then hesitated before saying, "It's ten o'clock. Time to feed the hens. Slide one of those feed bags over here." He pointed with his chin at the floor in front of him.

Although my brain was foggy, I knew I was in no position to argue. Deciding cooperation might earn some trust, I stepped over to the pile of feed bags, grabbed the burlap corners of the topmost bag, and yanked until I saw stars. The bag had barely budged. Across the bottom of the printed front, the words *60 LBS NET* told me what I had just learned: the bags wouldn't be easy to move.

After setting my feet and taking a big inhale, I heaved the bag harder, and this time, it slid toward me, gaining momentum as the bulk of it dropped off the pile and plunked on the floor.

With only a split second of warning, my stomach decided to reject all the water I had filled it with. As my brain realized what was happening, my eyes locked in on the bucket that was supposed to be my toilet. I took a step forward and dropped to my knees just in time to spew all that water into it.

After that one big gush, my eyeballs ached, and my head throbbed. I squeezed it at the temples while flies buzzed all around me, now drawn to the contents of the bucket: mostly water and bile, with a smattering of food remnants—a gross reminder I was due to eat, as horrible as the idea sounded in that moment.

As my stomach began settling, I collected myself, wiping my mouth and looking around, glad to find no evidence of stray puke outside the pail.

"Hand me that bucket."

I had almost forgotten about the man who had just watched me vomit.

"I'll rinse it out."

I rose to my feet and steadied myself against the whirling sensation, questioning whether it was the concussion, the exertion, or having downed too much water at once that had made me throw up. Probably all three, I concluded.

The moth took flight from the window, flitted around the room, then sailed out the open doorway. *Freedom. Must be nice,* I thought.

After making sure there was no vomit on the handle, I flipped it up, took hold, and carried it toward the door with my chain dragging behind me. As I approached, my captor stepped back from the doorway, making me wonder if he thought I might dump the contents on him. As tempting as it sounded, this wouldn't help.

When the chain started to tighten, I put the bucket down.

"Bring me the pitcher," he said. "I'll refill it."

The idea of drinking more water made me want to ralph all over again, but I knew I had to try, so I did as he asked.

After I placed it near the bucket, he nodded, then his eyes turned to the bag of chicken feed.

"Give me a minute," I said, leaning against my knees. "You gave me a concussion with that knock on the head."

I was pretty sure it was he who had done that, but his response confirmed it. "Sorry about that." His frown told me that maybe he even meant it.

Moving slowly, I went back to the bag. I found that if I leaned back and leveraged my weight, I could drag it across the floor. Until it snagged on something, that is. I yanked against the resistance, tearing a small hole in the bag, which freed it, but left a trail of chicken feed pellets in its wake.

"Those pesky mice get into everything," the man said.

I was working too hard to immediately understand he thought a mouse had chewed a hole in the bag, so I didn't bother correcting him.

"Or, it could be a rat," he added.

I shuddered at the thought, but remained quiet as I dragged the leaking bag over to the puke bucket. The old man stepped back once again, which seemed to confirm he was worried I might be a threat to him. Fat chance in my state, not to mention the chain holding me back.

He gave a little head toss in the direction of the back end of the room. "Sit down over there while I feed the hens."

Glad to get off my feet, I obeyed his order. I plopped down and leaned against the back wall with my legs outstretched.

"Don't move," he said as he reached for the bucket and placed it outside. He then stepped into the vestibule, walking sideways with the gun in both hands. I'm not sure what he was so jumpy about, because that stretch between the outside door and the door to where the hens were kept was beyond my reach. Most likely, he had planned it that way, fixing the chain at just the right point. Maybe he didn't trust his arithmetic. But I was beginning to see that this guy was a Nervous Nelly all around. I'd learned that term from Grandma.

When he pushed open the hen room door, the chickens clucked excitedly. *Bawwwk...bawk bawk bawk...bawwwk.*

He propped the gun inside, then hoisted the chicken feed bag up from the floor and onto his shoulder, looking like he might totter over. A steady stream of pellets spilled from the bag where I had torn it. He wobbled his way to the doorway, glancing back at me one last time to make sure I had stayed put before he disappeared from view.

A thump soon followed, which I felt through the floorboards.

By the time I realized he had dropped the bag, he peeked back through the doorway. Satisfied I hadn't moved, he went back to his hen feeding duties.

Maybe if my thinking hadn't been so cloudy, the idea would have come to me sooner. It wasn't until I distractedly traced the pellet trail from the doorway back to where it started that the thought struck me.

Chapter 9

As anxious as I was to see if my idea might work, I waited, knowing I had to be patient.

Eventually, the hen room door cracked open. The man peeked out at me, then slipped back into the vestibule with the half-empty feed bag, which he put in the corner.

He went back to retrieve the wire basket, now half-filled with eggs, and the gun, closing the hen door behind him. "I'll be back with the clean bucket and more water," he said, then headed out the main door.

Standing outside the doorway, he opened his mouth to say something, then closed it. He glanced at the house, then back at me. "What's your name?"

I wondered if maybe I shouldn't tell him my real name, then decided it didn't matter. "Emma Griffiths."

He rubbed his beard and repeated, "Emma." Then, he added. "I'm Eli. Eli Yoder."

I didn't know what to say in response. It wasn't going to be, "Nice to meet you."

He didn't wait for a reply anyway. He simply swung the door closed and bolted it.

I thought, *Really?* Locking the door while I was chained beyond its reach seemed like overkill.

Then, I added, *But maybe not for long.*

I resisted the urge to investigate my idea. Instead, I got up to watch him wander off. After he disappeared behind the house, I searched for other signs of movement, but all I saw was the clothing on the front porch clothesline fluttering in the wind.

With the sun high in the sky, I figured it was midday now. The chicken coop had gotten hotter, too. As I wiped the sweat off my face, I realized I had grown thirsty again.

I heard what I soon realized was one of those old iron well pumps cranking away.

When I was a kid, my grandparents would take me to a petting farm. The farm sold tickets that could be redeemed for cones of animal feed. The first time I fed one of those cones to a lamb, it bit my finger. I learned quickly to hold the cones from the bottom and to let go the instant the animals chomped down.

You could also trade a ticket for a bucket to be filled with well water, manually pumped with an old-fashioned hand pump. You'd pour the bucket into the animal's water troughs. The first few times I worked that pump, it was fun. But I soon realized it was nothing but a workout, and I was doing the farm's labor for them while paying for the privilege.

Judging by the sound I was hearing, it was clear that this farm had that same type of pump, although it wasn't a novelty here.

The cranking finished, and Eli soon reappeared, coming my way. I decided I should return to where he had last seen me, unsure whether he still expected me to stay put.

I was fully settled when the door swung open. This time, instead of the gun, he brought a whisk broom and a dustpan. It was the most enormous dustpan I'd ever seen. I guess it was a farm-sized dustpan.

He placed the pitcher of water on the floor, sloshing some out into a puddle in the process, then put the bucket beside it. Next, he pulled something out of his pocket, which he unfurled into a spiral ribbon, before stepping into the room.

"Since you didn't eat your breakfast, I can't bring a midday meal," he said as he hung the coil from one rafter. "They don't want food wasted."

There was that word again: *They.*

"I'll try to bring you supper, though. That is, if you want it."

I shrugged. I needed food, and I did feel hungry now, yet eating seemed so unimportant compared to the need to break free.

He stepped back from the spiral strip, now dangling from the rafter. It took me a moment to recognize it as one of those sticky fly-catcher tapes. I had always doubted those things made much of a difference, but I now found myself praying they did.

As he began sweeping the feed pellets into a pile, I asked myself, *Who is this guy? How is he related to the demonic woman?*

He left alone the first couple of feet of the pellet trail nearest me. I figured he left it because he thought he'd be getting too close. Whatever. I was glad.

After pushing the pile into that giant dustpan, he dumped it into the half-empty feed bag and headed for the door. "You should eat supper," he said.

Did he really care? I tried to read his expression, but I only got a quick glimpse of his face before he stepped out through the doorway, so who knows?

"Okay," I said, as he began swinging the door closed. He paused, nodded in acknowledgment, and then shut it with a slam.

After the deadbolt latched, I waited a minute, then peeked out the window in time to see him climb the front porch and disappear into the house, with the screen door banging behind him.

My back itched, so I did the bear scratch thing again, then went over to the water pitcher, squatted, and took a swig of the water.

Although it felt just as good going down my bone-dry throat once again, I told myself, *Pace yourself.* This time, I listened.

Next, I headed over to the spot where the bag had snagged on the floor and dropped to my knees. I opened my palm, laid it on the floor, and swept it over the area where the pellet trail started.

It didn't take long to find what I was looking for. I brushed the area clean and leaned forward, examining the nail head protruding ever so slightly above the board's surface. I slid my thumbnail underneath it, gauging the gap between the nail head and the wood to be thinner than a credit card. Not much to work with, but it was something.

The plank with the nail head poking up was two boards removed from the one anchoring my chain to the floor. Damn. It was a long shot, but I had hoped it was the same piece.

A thorough search of the floor for other nails that had worked their way up from the surface yielded only one, way back in the corner. That one wasn't going to do me any good.

Dragging my chain to the front of the room, I picked up the galvanized bucket. *My toilet,* I thought, then corrected myself. *No, hopefully, my pry tool.*

I examined the steel tabs riveted to the outside of the rim, each with a hole punched in it, through which the handle bail was wrapped. The steel was thick enough to provide some rigidity, but was it thin enough to fit under the nail head? I couldn't tell—only one way to find out.

But first, I checked out the window to see if the coast was clear. It was.

From my hands and knees, I attempted to insert the tab under the nail head. It was too thick. I tried the opposite tab and came in from different directions, but I got the same result each time. "Come on!" I whispered, shaking a fist at it.

Next, I tried chiseling into the wood with the corner of the tab and managed to shave out a few splinters, which I brushed clear. I checked again and could tell I was closer, so I went back at it.

After several minutes of gouging out fragments of wood, sweat was pouring off my face, leaving dark drips on the floorboards.

Lo and behold, on the next try, I managed to tuck the steel tab underneath the nail head.

My progress gave me an emotional boost. But since some time had passed, I forced myself to stop and check if anyone was coming. When I looked out the window, I immediately spotted movement.

My brothers were on the front porch, pulling clothes off the clothesline. Seeing them gave me some comfort, even though I had no way of knowing what they were going through.

Ungodly—I started thinking of that as the thing's nickname—stood near the doorway, overseeing their chores. Although I was in no mood to laugh about it, the irony of this wasn't lost on me. My brothers were highly skilled at avoiding household chores, despite Mom's—and my—best efforts. But here they were, acting like dedicated domestic helpers.

They each took one end of the last thing hanging, a bedsheet, pulled it down, then folded it and laid it in a basket at the woman's feet. She lifted the basket and led the way into the house. Just like that, they were gone.

I looked back at the part of the floor I was working on and suddenly felt it was too risky to continue. If Eli popped in, I'd have little time to hide what I was doing.

Should I wait until nighttime? Except, it would be dark then, and I doubted I'd be given candles or an oil lamp.

I decided to wait until dinnertime. *Suppertime,* I corrected—as he had called it. I blew away the wood splinters, spread the pellets around to cover my worksite, then placed the bucket next to the pitcher.

My stomach hadn't vomited the water this time, so I took a few more drinks before sitting on the floor, leaning against the four remaining feed bags.

Rubbing the welt on the back of my head, I wondered if the swelling had gone down. It seemed like it might have, although I understood the effects of the concussion could linger for a couple of days or more.

I found that if I reclined a certain way, I could settle into a comfortable position with no pressure on the wound.

Lying there gave me a direct view of that flycatcher, which already had several black dots sticking to it. It twirled lazily under the rafters, creating a hypnotic effect.

Despite what had become a stifling heat and the nightmare I was living through, exhaustion overcame me, and I fell asleep.

Chapter 10

A rattling sound jarred me awake, which I figured out was the door lock.

As I blinked the sleep away, I noticed the shadows in the room had shifted. The twirling spiral ribbon caught my eye. It was dotted with dozens of flies now, although others still buzzed around me.

The door swung out, revealing Eli holding a plate of food. He placed it on the floor and slid it toward me. "Do you need your outhouse emptied?"

I had to think about what that meant, but then it came to me. When I shook my head, I must have done it too quickly, because the movement triggered a woozy sensation.

"You should drink more water," he said.

I looked at the pitcher, which remained more than half full, and suddenly felt thirsty. I tried licking my parched lips, but that did little good because my tongue was just as dry. Eli was right.

The good news was the room didn't seem as hot anymore. Or maybe I was getting used to it.

"Are my brothers okay?" The question spilled out without my even thinking of it.

The old man gave me a long look. He cleared his throat, said, "I'll be back after supper," then closed and bolted the door.

He left so abruptly, I didn't know what to read into it. It told me I had to come through for my brothers, though.

I pushed up onto my feet and waited for the room to stop spinning. When it did, I went over to the window and watched Eli climb the porch and disappear into the house. *Bang* went the screen door. Apparently, his mother had never taught him not to slam the door.

Stooping down next to the pitcher, I lifted it to my face and took a few long gulps. Once again, I reminded myself not to overdo it and made sure to follow my own advice.

I poured some into my hand and splashed it over my face, savoring the cool feeling, then stood and returned to the window.

For a long minute, I switched my gaze between the plate of food, the spot on the floor with the jutting nail head, and outside, at the house. Flies were swarming the food, which I knew I needed to eat. I was ravenous, but also nauseated by the sight of it.

Then there was the question of whether now was a good time to work on the nail. Would they be eating supper? Maybe not yet. I decided to eat first, making sure they had settled into their meal before resuming work on the floorboard.

I took another drink before dragging the chain across the floor to get the plate of food.

Sitting on the stack of feed bags, I rested the plate on my lap and looked over its contents: mashed potatoes, roasted chicken, and green beans. A home-cooked meal if ever there was one.

I wondered if my brothers would be eating the same thing. They probably would, I figured. They both *hated* green beans. At least, they did in their normal state of mind.

Using my fork, I first scraped off a chunk of mashed potatoes and sniffed, then nibbled on it, assessing whether any strange odors or flavors didn't belong. It tasted delicious.

Knowing how long my stomach had been empty, I tried not to devour the food quickly. I also made a point of chewing it well, so it would be easier to digest.

While I munched, the flies took a strong interest in my plate, so I had to keep shooing them away.

Ordinarily, a glass of milk would have gone well with this meal, but Eli hadn't brought me that. I guess he figured I had plenty of water to drink. But since he hadn't even given me a glass for the water, I had to take a couple of breaks to wash down the food with swigs from the pitcher.

My gaze kept drifting down to the feed pellets covering the nail head. Anxious to get started, I told myself to finish dinner first—and for the sake of my stomach, not to rush it.

Before starting, I wasn't sure if I'd be able to eat it all, but as it turned out, I did. As soon as I finished, though, my stomach felt like it might burst. It seemed as if I had scarfed down four plates, probably because it had been so long since I'd last eaten.

I put the plate near the door and went over to look out the window. The sky remained clear, but the bright glare was gone because the sun had shifted behind the trees, shading the henhouse. Seeing no movement, I decided this was my chance.

I took the bucket over to the hidden nail head, got on my knees, and wiped the pellet pile aside.

As soon as my fingers brushed over the tiny projection, my heart started racing. I blew the nail head clear and, with my hands shaking, tucked the steel lip underneath. So far, so good. But when I twisted the bucket, the nail didn't budge—instead, the lip bent.

I let out a groan and slammed a fist against my thigh. Twisting the opposite way, it simply bent back. "Damn it!" I whispered out loud, rolling the bucket over to try again using the opposite side.

Tucking it under the nail head, I told myself to be more careful. If I pried slowly and directed the force into the nail instead of the steel I was prying with, maybe I'd get a better result. But when I twisted and lifted, that side gave just the same.

Driven partly by frustration and not stopping to think things through, I gave it a sharp twist, and the tab broke free from the bucket. I shook my head, wondering how I would explain the busted handle to Eli.

As I stared at it, a new thought came to me. The hole in the newly freed tab that the handle looped through was elongated, so I bent the tab in the middle of the hole, where it was weakest, and wrapped it around the nail head, increasing my grip on it.

The handle provided me with an easy way to tug. With one yank, the nail came straight out of the ancient floorboard.

I couldn't believe my luck. Finally, something had gone my way.

When I looked the nail over, a different idea came to me. I contorted my arms behind my back and tried sticking the pointy end into the padlock. It's not like I had ever picked a lock before, but I figured it was worth a try. The nail was a little too thick, though, so I couldn't even get it into the keyhole. With a huff, I redirected my efforts to the floorboards.

Suddenly, I heard the front screen door bang, sending me into a panic. With little time to think, I tucked the nail under the bottom feed bag and swept the loose pellets over the floorboard hole.

I moved the bucket next to the pitcher, resting the handle on the lip and hiding the broken tab on the back, then hurried to the stack of feed bags. By the time the lock started rattling, I had already climbed back on top.

The door swung out, revealing Eli without his straw hat, putting his greasy, gray hair on full display. I tried to look relaxed, which wasn't easy with my shaking hands and heavy breathing.

As he looked around, I gritted my teeth, convinced I had left something out of place. When his eyes locked on the bucket, my heart seemed to quit beating. It took everything in me to avoid looking at it, afraid I'd see the detached handle hanging free.

"Need your outhouse emptied?"

"No," I said, maybe a bit too quickly. It was a good thing I hadn't used the bucket for that yet, although I had the feeling it wouldn't be long before I would.

He nodded, then leaned forward and grabbed my empty plate.

"Need more water?"

I looked at the pitcher, still half full, and shook my head.

Eli shrugged, stepped back from the door, swung it closed, then set the deadbolt.

I stayed frozen on the feed bag, my heart thumping in my ears, listening for the screen door. As soon as I heard it, I rushed over to the window to make sure no one was wandering around. Seeing no sign of life, I went back to the floor.

I tried to pull the floorboard up, clamping it on the edges with my fingertips. It didn't budge. Next, I tried wiggling it from side to side. Nothing. It seemed glued down.

I fished the nail out from under the feed sack and examined it. Not much longer than my thumb, the metal was smooth and the point sharp. I stabbed it into the gap at the end of the board it had come from. The soft wood splintered as I worked it in, digging the tip downward with a back-and-forth motion.

After embedding the tip as far as it would go, I pressed on the nail to pry the board up. At first, all that happened was that the board

I was leveraging against split, and the nail sank into the crack. But eventually, the nail met solid resistance. With one last pry, the board suddenly broke free from the years of crud holding it down.

Now, I needed to lever the second nail out.

I tried grasping the plank with my fingertips, but I only managed to raise it a fraction of an inch before I lost my grip. The board sprang back down with a thwack.

Blowing out a long, exasperated breath, I sat back on my heels and wiped my open hands over my face, trying to clear my mind. It must have helped, because another idea came to me.

I crawled over to grab the pail. Once again, I used the nail to pry the board back up, but this time, I jabbed the steel tab that had detached from the bucket's lip into the end of the board to hold it in place. I then dug the nail in lower to lever the plank higher, and repeated the pattern, working the piece of wood up by switching between the nail and the steel tab.

Soon, I had raised the end of the floorboard above those on either side, so I held it there while I slid the bucket's wire handle underneath, propping it up.

My small victory had me wanting more, but I knew not to push my luck. I hurried over to the window and peeked out. Since the coast was still clear, I went back to work.

I tried yanking the floorboard out with the bucket handle, but it was so thin it dug into my fingers. Needing something thicker to shove underneath the plank, my mind settled on the chain I was tethered to.

I snaked it over, arranging it on the floor just past the end of the board. Using the handle to lift the plank, I slid my knee under one end of the handle, then used my free hand to push the chain underneath. When I let go, the floorboard settled on top of the chain.

The entire ordeal left me feeling lightheaded, so I took a quick break to nurse my sore fingers while taking a few long drinks from the pitcher.

I would have gotten up to check out the window, but the free part of my leash was now half its length, so it couldn't reach. I was flying blind; I had to settle for the slamming screen door as my warning signal.

"Okay, let's get going," I whispered to myself, putting down the pitcher and rising to my feet.

Standing over the floorboard, I braced my feet shoulder-width apart, grasped the chain on either side of the plank, and tugged as if I were doing dumbbell rows.

The floorboard groaned as it bent. When it gave a little, I almost lost my balance, but I recovered and yanked harder.

The nail screeched as it began separating from the floor joist, before popping out entirely.

With the leash slackened to normal length once more, I glanced out the window to confirm that no one was in sight.

The sun had dropped low in the sky, which told me it would be getting dark before long. I not only had to worry about getting caught, but I also had limited daylight left.

It took me a few minutes to remove the nail from the freed plank, giving me one loose floorboard and two loose nails.

The bad news was that I had two more boards to remove before I'd be free, and I would soon run out of sunlight. Not only that, if I had to guess, Eli would be checking on me even sooner.

To top it all off, I needed to use the outhouse.

Using a bucket as a toilet was as bad as I thought. No, it was even worse.

There was nothing to wipe with or wash my hands with. When I was finished, I rinsed my hands and poured some of the water into the bucket, hoping this would reduce the smell. It didn't seem to help much.

I moved the bucket as close to the door as I could reach and rinsed my hands again with the last of the water, then went back to the task of freeing myself.

I stuck my fingers into the opening where the plank had been and grasped the next floorboard. Although I gave it a hard yank, it didn't budge. There was no way I was going to pry out that plank with my bare hands.

Resting my palms on my thighs, I blew out a long breath while my gaze drifted down into the dimly lit space below the gap.

My heart seized. I leaned forward and squinted, straining to adjust my eyesight to the darkness. Praying I wasn't seeing what I thought I was seeing, I blinked.

But the image was clear, so I couldn't deny it.

Underneath the chicken coop, the ground was covered with bones.

CHAPTER 11

WITH MY HAND CLASPED over my mouth, I tried to tell myself, *It could be animal bones*.

Until the human skull staring back at me through the pile told me, *Quit fooling yourself!*

It took everything in me to stay calm. I would have screamed, but I felt like the wind had been knocked out of me. I would have run away, but the shackles wouldn't have it.

All I could do was cover the hole back up.

I grabbed the floorboard and attempted to insert it where it had been, but one end was too thick to fit. *How is that possible?* I frantically asked before realizing I had to turn it the other way around, fumbling it in the process. Eventually, it dropped into the gap, like the final piece of a jigsaw puzzle.

Hiding the bones brought me the tiniest sliver of relief. But whose skeletons were they? How many dead people were hidden down there? I had only seen one skull, but I could only see through a little sliver, and there were way too many bones for just one person. How long had they been there? How did they die?

I tried to push the unanswerable questions out of my mind and concentrate on putting the place back in order before Eli returned.

A dark hole stood out on either end of the floorboard, in place of the missing nails. In an attempt to hide them, I brushed dirt over the top, then ground it into the openings with my fingertip. It helped quite a bit. I told myself that at his age, Eli's eyesight wouldn't be good enough to spot the holes and moved on.

After recreating the chicken feed trail, I searched for a good hiding place for the nails. I found an extra-wide crevice between the wall and the flooring underneath the window, long and deep enough to tuck them into, end to end. They remained visible, but I had the elderly eyesight thing working in my favor, not to mention the fading daylight.

Standing up, I peered out the window in time to see Eli's shadow step out onto the porch. The screen door banged behind him.

Without waiting to see if he was heading my way, I scrambled back to the feed bags, took a seat, and tried to slow my breathing down. It wasn't long before the lock began its familiar rattle.

The door swung open, revealing Eli with his gun.

I watched him, expecting he'd react to the smell. Under normal circumstances, I would have died of embarrassment. But I was way past the point of caring about trivial things like that. My main concern was that he might notice something out of place.

He scanned the room, then shifted his gun into one hand while reaching for the bucket. Of course, when he tried to swing the handle up, the detached end flopped free. He looked at it, then at me, then back at it.

"What happened here?" he said, feeling the steel tab with his fingertips.

I shrugged and said in the most casual tone I could manage, "The handle came off when I lifted it." Afraid he might hear the tremble in my voice, I left it at that.

He turned the pail around and examined where the tab had been spot-welded, rubbing it with his thumb. After clearing his throat, he took hold of the pail by the rim and moved it outside.

"Can you hand me that pitcher?"

Glad I no longer had to sit there faking being relaxed, I slid off the feed bag and did as he asked.

Eli stepped back as I carried the pitcher toward him, and when I put it down, he nodded. "I'll bring you a couple of horse blankets. They'll make a good bed."

I turned away so he couldn't see me roll my eyes in response.

He waited for me to go back to the other end of the room before grabbing the pitcher and closing the door. Sure enough, he bolted it.

I crawled back onto the feedbags and hugged my knees, fully conscious of the pile of bones under the floor. As dumb as it sounds, it somehow felt as though the bags gave me more distance from them.

Before I became aware I was trapped above skeletons, I had felt my captivity couldn't get any worse. How stupid of me.

A few minutes later, the well pump cranked.

An orangish glow streamed through the window, telling me the sun was setting. I considered the prospect of spending the night in this dark room with human remains underneath me. This got me freaking out so badly I could no longer breathe steadily.

I wasn't sure what upset me more: having human skeletons so close by, or knowing others like me—and maybe my brothers—had ended up there. Probably both.

When Eli reopened the door, he was balancing a stack of blankets on one arm with the pitcher in his other hand. After putting the pitcher down, he shook the blankets off, dropping them into a pile on the floor, revealing a different bucket hanging under the crook of his arm.

I thought, *A wooden bucket? Do they still even make those things?* Probably not. With the wood all beaten up and faded, held together with rusty metal staves, it looked like an antique.

"I'll need to fix that other pail," he said, sliding the wooden one toward me.

My paranoid brain wondered if he had switched to this one because he suspected I couldn't be trusted with the metal one.

"We rise with the sun. Will you eat breakfast?"

I nodded while thinking about how, with any luck, I would *not* be eating that breakfast.

Eli rubbed his beard and squinted at me. I looked away to keep him from reading anything in my eyes that would tell him I was up to something.

After a while, he pulled the door closed without a word, and the room turned shockingly dark.

I waited for a minute after the lock clicked, then slipped off the feed bags. I tiptoed over to the window, although I'm not sure why I felt I should be quiet. Maybe deep down inside, I was afraid I'd disturb the skeletons' spirits.

Outside, it was turning dusk. One of the home's open windows glowed weakly from an oil lamp. Eli's shadowy figure lingered on the porch while he petted Sonny. He rose and headed into the house. *Slam* went the screen door.

I blew out a long breath and rested my forehead against the windowsill. *That's it,* I told myself. Since there was no way I was going to open up that floorboard in the dark, I would be spending the night here. Alone. Just me, the hens, and some human remains.

"Might as well try to get comfortable," I whispered. "While there's still enough light to see my way around."

I inspected the wooden bucket. It too had a wire bale with a wooden handle in the middle. The ends were attached with steel fasteners, which appeared to be screwed into the wood. It might be possible to pry them out with my nails, but it was too dark to tell for sure. I'd need to look again when daylight returned. Anyway, they didn't look as useful for prying as the steel tabs on the last bucket had been.

What looked more promising were the three metal staves, although in the dim light, I couldn't tell how well they were secured.

I moved the bucket to its corner along with the pitcher, which I forced myself to take a few long swigs out of.

There were four bags of chicken feed left on the stack, so I pulled them off and butted them against one another, forming a sort of mattress. As I moved around, I was careful to avoid stepping on the loose floorboard, which might jar it out of place, opening a passageway between the pile of bones and my room.

Next, I spread the blankets over the makeshift mattress for a little extra padding, figuring it was too warm to cover myself anyway. I placed the feather in the corner, thinking maybe it would protect me. Like the dreamcatcher I had hanging on my headboard at home.

When I lay down in the bed, I was surprised to see it wasn't as uncomfortable as I had expected. I'm sure it helped that I had done my share of tent sleeping without an air mattress.

I bunched up the blankets to form a pillow of sorts and rested my head against it. I couldn't lie on my back because of the chain and the padlock, not to mention the lump on the back of my head. That was okay because I tend to sleep on my sides anyway.

It wasn't fully dark yet, so I think that made me comfortable closing my eyes. I didn't expect to do much sleeping, but I somehow managed to fall asleep almost right away.

CHAPTER 12

I AWAKENED WITH A jolt, startled by a deep rumble. My mind immediately recognized where I was and, in an instant, veered to the skeletons.

The bones had rattled. I was convinced of it.

I sat up, rubbed my eyes, and looked around, but could see almost nothing in the nearly pitch-black room.

What would I do with skeletons moving around underneath me? My pulse quickened at the thought of it. What *could* I do?

Straining to listen, I tuned my ears.

Then it sounded again. No, it was just thunder, off in the distance. My panic subsided a bit.

I wondered how long I had slept. Maybe not long. Then again, maybe hours had passed. I had no way of knowing.

Light flashed in the window, followed by another crack of thunder, louder this time.

I had to pee, so I scooted over to the edge of my mattress, rolled onto my knees, and pushed onto my feet.

Staring at the section near the loosened floorboard, I wanted to make sure it was still in place. But it was so dark, I couldn't tell. *Forget about it,* I told myself, sidestepping the area.

I had to feel around to find the bucket. My outhouse, as Eli would have called it.

When I finished, I felt around blindly for the pitcher and made myself drink some water before shuffling over to the window.

The sky had clouded over, blocking the stars and moonlight, so I could barely even make out the faint form of the house.

When lightning flashed, I gasped and jerked back. It was the briefest moment, but what I saw made me want to shriek.

A figure crouched on the roof of the house.

I had gotten a profile view of the figure, dressed in black, its head cocked skyward. The ungodly one—I was sure of it.

I staggered back from the window as I felt the blood drain out of my face. With the horrifying image etched in my brain, I pressed my palms against my temples and squeezed.

Could I have imagined it?

How could I? *My frazzled mind is playing tricks on me,* I reasoned.

Lightning flashed again, revealing the dreadful sight of her once more, licking the air with that inhumanly overstretched tongue.

Thunder clapped, then faded into silence.

Although I didn't want to see any more, I couldn't look away. Frozen in place, I stood there on wobbly knees, panting as if hyperventilating, watching for another burst of light.

What happened next added stupor to my terror.

Lightning struck *her.*

The bolt zigzagged down from the sky, bending to reach her, then arcing down the side of the house. The flash was so bright it blinded me; the nearly simultaneous crash of thunder so deafening it rocked the chicken coop.

What just happened? a frantic voice inside my head asked. *Did you really see that?* I knew I wasn't dreaming because everything was all too vivid.

But maybe it was a delusion. Maybe I was losing my grip on sanity.

I needed to see her again. I told myself there was no way anyone could survive a direct strike like that, wanting to believe she hadn't. *Please,* I prayed, *show me her. Show me she's dead.*

Lightning flashed, illuminating the scene once again. Ungodly remained upright, smoldering, no longer licking the air, but with her arms raised.

"No, no, no," I whimpered under my breath. Being struck hadn't *killed* her; it had *energized* her.

The following span of darkness stretched way too long, but when the next flash of light finally came, the most spine-chilling image yet appeared: Ungodly, crawling down the side of the house.

Headfirst...like a spider.

I clasped my hand over my mouth to stifle a scream.

Another blaze of light came a few seconds later, but she was already gone.

Where is she?

I pictured her creeping outside the henhouse.

All of a sudden, everything felt too quiet.

Straining to stay upright, I stepped back further from the window, keeping clear of the loose floorboard area.

Another image formed inside my mind: that impossibly long tongue poking up from below, pushing the loose plank out, licking the interior air like a snake.

With my heart pounding frantically, I hopped onto the feedbag bed.

As if I were on the verge of suffocating, my breath came out in uneven wheezes. Surrounded by an awful, dark void, I pulled myself into a seated fetal position, bear-hugging my knees, and begged for another flash of lightning.

When it came, I saw that the board remained in place. *See?* I said to myself as the thunder pealed. *Don't imagine things.*

As I tried to ease myself out of runaway panic, the clouds opened up, pummeling the structure imprisoning me, while the wind rattled the siding.

The racket did nothing to help calm me down, because it got me thinking that if that being *were* sneaking around outside—or if the bones beneath me *were* rattling—there was no way I'd ever hear it.

Maybe the worst part was not knowing where to direct my fear: outside? Or under the floor?

After each lightning strike, I'd anxiously wait in the pitch blackness for another, fully expecting the next flash of light to reveal Ungodly inside the room with me.

Over the next few minutes, the downpour intensified. I trembled, feeling as though *I* were being shaken. My body started to ache.

As the rain pelted the metal roof, another mind-numbing idea came to me. Could any of those sounds be her, crawling *above* me? I pictured her lurking up there, creeping ever closer.

The thought of Ungodly slithering around on the henhouse roof became too much, and I finally melted down. I cried like I've never cried before, falling into a tailspin of hysterics, not holding back, since I couldn't even hear myself over the hellacious storm.

I wept intensely, with the horror of the moment supercharged by the release of all the pent-up dread, hurt, and anger that had built up inside me.

Overwhelmed with that surge of emotions, I began asking myself if I could be having a mental breakdown. It certainly felt like it.

The goal of getting us out of this ever-worsening nightmare seemed hopeless. In that moment, I became nothing but a vulnerable baby. All I could do was bawl my eyes out.

As the thunder and lightning carried on, their effect gradually began to dull. It was like the fear had been wrung out of me. I started crying myself out, sinking into a pattern of shaking, strangled sobs.

I embraced this weariness and instead strained to think happy thoughts. With one flash of light, I glimpsed the carnival glass pitcher, which brought Mom, Grandma, and my great-grandmother to mind. I thought about home. Our dog, Bluey. My friends. What it would be like when I head off to college in a few weeks...if I make it out of here, that is.

I caught myself tracing the letters on my ALS bracelet, but told myself to stop. Of all things, I couldn't let my thoughts fall on Dad.

As the storm raged on, I remained pinned to the feed-bag mattress, avoiding looking out the window. If that figure was out there, I didn't want to see it. Chained up as I was, what could I do about it anyway? I was better off not knowing.

My hands began to throb. I realized I had clenched them into tight fists, with my nails digging into my palms. As I opened my fingers and splayed them out to release the tension, I noticed the rain was letting up, and the thunder was getting quieter.

I told myself to stop blubbering like a child and wiped my cheeks dry, then picked up the feather and brushed it against my arms and legs, hoping the silky feeling might soothe my tattered psyche.

I'm not sure if the feather made much difference, but my nerves began settling with the passing of the storm. It felt like it had raged on for hours, but in reality, it was probably more like half an hour.

A while later, the wind died down, the rain stopped altogether, and the thunder faded to distant rumbles.

With the feather clutched in my hand, I lay back on the bed, trying not to listen for sounds outside.

I kept telling myself to focus on my happy thoughts instead. It must have helped, because somewhere along the line, exhaustion reached its tipping point, and my weary mind drifted off into sleep.

Chapter 13

My eyes snapped open at the racket of a rooster crowing in the distance.

The sound of birds singing filled my ears. I blinked the sleep away and looked at the window. The sun hadn't risen yet, but the sky was turning gray.

There was already enough light in the room that I could see my surroundings. My eyes shot over to the floorboard. It remained in place.

I pushed myself upright and sat cross-legged on the makeshift mattress. The feather rested on the edge of the horse blanket, where I had apparently dropped it in my sleep.

I could still feel the bruise on my back from that fall, but it wasn't as bad. My head didn't hurt as much either, and the knot where I'd been clubbed wasn't as swollen.

I stretched, then rose and went to the window. On instinct, my eyes homed in on the roof. It was empty.

I looked around, thinking I might spot my brothers in the garden, but there was no sign of life. Even the dog—Sonny—was nowhere to be seen. Maybe with the rain, he had slept in the barn.

The heat of the past two days was gone now, telling me the storm had been a passing cold front.

I took a long drink of water, then poured some into my palm to rinse my face. God, how I wished I had soap. Shampoo. A toothbrush and toothpaste. I cut myself off, knowing that self-pity would do me no good.

I had to pee, so I wasted no time in taking care of business. Since I had also gone during the night, I took this as a sign I wasn't as dehydrated anymore. Even so, I drank some more water, to be sure.

Back at the window, I watched for movement while planning out my next steps. Eli would be coming, but when? "We rise with the sun," he had said. The sun would rise soon, but if yesterday were any indication, he wouldn't be visiting until breakfast was cooked. He had also told me that he fed the hens at ten o'clock, which would be even later.

So, I had some time, but how much? Most likely, no more than an hour. Was that enough? I wasn't sure. What I *was* sure of was that I had to get out of here, and the sooner, the better. So, I went to work.

Crouching down, I used my thumbnail to poke the sharp ends of each nail, pivoting the opposite ends out of their hiding crevice.

On my knees beside the loose floorboard, I swept the trail of chicken feed clear and used the nails to lever the loose board up. I didn't want to look down there, but I forced myself to. With the sun coming up, I had enough daylight to see the jumble of shadows. I watched for a moment, making sure the bones weren't moving. They weren't.

Still, the sight of them crippled me. The flood of questions came rushing back. How many skeletons were down there? When did they die? *How* did they die? My body shuddered, breaking my paralysis.

Then, I noticed something. I leaned in closer, squinting. Underneath the floor, light spilled in from the perimeter of the crawlspace.

Meaning the chicken coop was built on an open foundation, which provided a possible escape route.

But first things first. I had to free the chain from the floorboard.

I crawled over to the bucket and looked it over. The wire handle was attached with flimsy-looking fasteners, with two screws securing each side to the wood. Nails held the staves in place, but they couldn't have been long; otherwise, they would have poked through the inside of the pail.

I pushed myself onto my feet, picked up the bucket, and carried it over to the opening in the floor. "Sorry," I whispered. "I don't mean any disrespect, but I need this pail, and there's no place else to dump it." I tilted the bucket over and poured my urine down the hole. The heap of bones softened the splashing sound.

When the pail was empty, I laid it on its side in the middle of the floor. I sucked in a big breath, braced myself, and stomped on it.

My kick did nothing to the bucket, but the impact carried through my body, re-triggering my headache.

After waiting for my head to clear, I lifted the length of chain off the floor and grasped it in both hands, then hopped onto the bucket, landing on it with both feet, kicking downward as I made contact.

The wood splintered with a muted crack, giving way under one foot but not the other. I toppled over and crashed to the floor. Lying on my side, I gave a victorious fist shake at the busted pail, while the hens clucked at the commotion.

I scrambled back to my feet and checked out the window. Although I doubted the sound of my fall could be heard from within the house, it would have been a different story if someone were outside. For the time being, the coast was clear.

I went back at it with a single foot stomp. After a few more solid kicks, the bucket was in pieces. The handle and its flimsy fasteners looked useless, so I set them aside, along with the fragments of wood. It was the staves I was after, those steel bands binding the wooden slats into the pail's round shape.

My kicks had loosened the small nails holding the staves to the wood, so I wiggled them out one at a time, dropping them into the hole in the floor. Each one gave a soft *ting* sound when it fell onto the bones.

The staves were bent out of shape from my kicks, but the rivets that formed them into a loop still held. One of them seemed looser than the others, so I focused on that one, bending the joint back and forth, feeling it loosen further with each twist. After half a dozen bends, one rivet broke free. A few more, and the other snapped off, too.

Even though it was early on a cooler day, I had to pause and wipe the sweat off my face.

I uncurled the band of steel as well as I could with my hands, then laid it on the floor and pushed onto my feet. After another glance out the window, I went back to work, stepping on the steel to straighten it further.

After a couple of minutes, I ran my hands over the band and decided it was straight enough. With any luck, the steel was thick enough to provide the rigidity I would need.

I got back on my knees and went to work on the next floorboard, stabbing the two nails I had removed the night prior between the board and the joist it sat on. Using the plank I had already freed, I tapped the nails in, then tried to pry the board up with them.

At first, the wood just splintered, but I kept at it and eventually gained enough solid leverage to jimmy the nail up. I wedged the steel band under the floorboard. After a few good twists, the nail was loose enough that I could grab the board and yank, raising it further with each upward jerk.

The last tug popped the nail free altogether. I took it out, dropped it next to the two others, and snaked the chain under the loose end, following the same trick I had used the day before.

Holding the chain looped around the board with both hands, I planted my feet and tugged. The board groaned as it bent. When I leaned back and pulled harder, the second nail released, giving a glorious creak as it came free from the joist.

My stoked mood soured instantly when I looked down into the widened gap in the floor and saw the empty eye socket of a second skull staring back. I jumped to my feet and stepped clear. With my hands cupped over my mouth, I took three deep, calming breaths and tried to put it out of my mind.

I peeked out the window and confirmed there was still no one in sight.

Although I had no time to waste, I paused to assess my progress. My chain was attached to the third and last plank. Should I keep at it? Or, was I pushing my luck?

The safe bet would have been to hide what I had been doing, but then it dawned on me that this wasn't an option, with the bucket in pieces. I could drop the wood fragments into the hole before replacing the floorboards, but Eli would notice it was missing. I kicked myself for not seeing this in advance, but decided the concussion still left me scatterbrained.

I was past the point of no return. I had to keep going, and with time running short, I had to hurry.

I went to work on the third floorboard, prying first with the nails, then the steel band, and finally the chain. With a satisfying creak, I pried the board—and myself—free.

"Yes, yes, yes!" I said under my breath, flipping the board over to examine the U-bolt.

Rust coated the tightly cranked-down nuts, telling me the chain I was attached to had been anchored a long time ago. I groaned, realizing that years or decades before, the skeletons had most likely been shackled the same way.

I told myself to concentrate on my escape plan and quit wasting time.

After taking a minute to back the second nail out from the plank my chain was attached to, I scrambled to the entrance of the hen's room. They clucked in unison as I swung open the door, parting to let me in.

This room was larger, with three windows, but each was the same tiny size as the one in the vestibule. The rafters and the roof were also built the same way, so I saw no way out through the top.

I returned to the smaller room and tugged on the doorknob of the main entrance. Nothing budged. It was a heavy door, a solid frame, and a tight deadbolt.

With a sigh, I went back to the hole in the floor and dropped to my knees.

Now that I had the tools and a system for removing the planks, each was coming out more quickly. Gauging how wide they were, it seemed that removing four more would open a wide enough hole in the floor to fit through.

Underneath, the gap between the bones and the joists was tall enough to squeeze under, but just thinking about having to army crawl over those bones made my blood curdle.

The home's screen door slammed, sending me into a panic. Although I was no longer attached to the floor, I had no time to leave through the crawlspace or any other way, and no time to prepare for the old man's arrival.

I turned one way, then the other, losing a few precious seconds while my frantic mind groped for a plan, only to come up empty. Until my eyes fixed on the pitcher of water, that is.

I lifted the chain so it wouldn't drag on the floor, grabbed the pitcher, and dumped its contents onto the bones. I positioned myself inside the door and laid the chain at my side.

My chest thudded, feeling like it was about to burst open.

Grasping the pitcher by the handle with one hand, I wrapped my other hand around the pouring lip and hooked my thumb over the rim. I raised the pitcher over my head, took a heavy breath, and turned myself into a statue.

The next few seconds felt like minutes. My arms shook as the lock rattled and the deadbolt released.

With my jaw clenched, I wound back my arms, the way Dad taught me to swing an axe. Knowing my window of opportunity would be short, I had to time it perfectly.

The door swung open, and the instant I saw Eli standing there holding a plate of food, I lunged forward. At first, he wore a blank expression, but his eyes shot open, and his jaw dropped in surprise. If he had an extra millisecond, he might have cried out, but I didn't give him that chance.

As I launched out the open doorway, I swung the pitcher down, but somehow Eli ducked, so the bottom edge of the pitcher barely glanced the crown of his head. I couldn't believe it; his reflexes were quicker than I had expected.

Not quick enough to duck out of my path, though. I crashed into him, knocking him backward. He crumpled underneath me, coughing out a grunt as my full weight landed on him.

When I came to rest, sprawled out on the still-damp grass, my legs were all tangled in the chain tethered to my back.

I turned to look at Eli, writhing on the ground behind me. He had taken a good pounding; for me, his body had softened the blow, like those foam landing pits we trained on in gymnastics.

I was still holding the pitcher by its handle, so I shook my legs free from the chain, scrambled onto my knees, and speed-crawled over to him. With both hands, I raised the pitcher over my head, closed my eyes, and smashed it into his forehead, my rage driving it like a battering ram.

His skull cracked. I felt it give way through the pitcher in my hands, and heard the gruesome sound of bone shattering, muffled under his flesh. With my eyes still squeezed shut, I forced myself to smack him again, overcoming my revulsion and a thread of remorse. The second strike felt mushy.

I pushed my eyes open to see what damage I'd done. A gush of blood oozed out from under his bangs. His mouth had gone slack, revealing several gaps between his remaining brown teeth.

My stomach did a flip when I saw blood smudges on the pitcher. I flung it on the ground as if it were too hot to touch, and recoiled. But then I noticed red polka dots on my shirt. Realizing they were blood splatters, I groaned and tried brushing them off, which only smeared them.

Since Eli wasn't moving, I rolled into a sitting position and took a moment to see if I had been injured. I felt dazed, but when I moved each limb, I had no major pain.

It didn't feel real to be free, like it was too good to be true. But I couldn't think that way, with my brothers still under Ungodly's spell.

I climbed to my feet and looked around. Over on the porch, Sonny was sitting upright, eyeing me with his head cocked. I could have laughed. Apparently, he wasn't overly concerned about his master.

I looked past Sonny at the house. The windows facing me were all open. Curtains shifted with the breeze, but there was no movement. Maybe Ungodly hadn't heard the scuffle.

Before turning back to Eli, I noticed a heavy, braided copper cable running down the side of the house, like the kind used to ground lightning rods. But there were no lightning rods mounted on the roof's ridge, where the cable ended abruptly. With a shudder, I tore my gaze away.

Eli was completely still. An inner voice told me he might just be unconscious, so maybe I should choke him with the chain. The idea made me want to retch, though, so I swept it away, telling myself I needed to get going with saving my brothers.

My chain stretched across Eli. The board attached to the opposite end sat on the stone step to the henhouse. I reeled it in, but the piece of wood caught on his hip. When I gave it an extra hard tug to free it, he rolled a bit, but settled right away.

Seeing how the jostling action hadn't roused him made me feel better, but having observed how the board could catch on something, I knew it had to go.

Eli's shirt had no pockets, but there was one on each side of his pants. The idea of touching this man made me sick, but I forced myself to check them, hoping to find the padlock key. Both pockets were empty.

But how had he unlocked the door? When I looked at the deadbolt, I found that the key was still inserted, although no other keys were attached. I'd have to wear the chain, but I could lose the board through brute force.

I propped the slat between the ground and the coop's sandstone step. I gathered the chain, pressed one foot above the U-bolt, then hopped on the opposite side with my other foot, coming down with my full weight on it. The board cracked and broke, splintering where the U-bolt had been attached.

As I wiggled the loose fragments free from the U-bolt, I noticed sections of lattice panel tucked along the perimeter, which I realized concealed the crawlspace where the bones lay. I stumbled back, hurrying away from the barely covered opening.

After looping the chain over my neck twice so the loose end wouldn't drag on the ground, I took one last look at Eli to triple-check that he remained still and headed for my first stop: the barn.

Chapter 14

THE BARN DOOR WAS cracked open just wide enough for me to get through.

I slipped into the dark interior and bumped into a wheel of the parked buggy. Feeling with my hands, I sidestepped around it on the packed dirt floor while waiting for my eyes to adjust.

A small window at the back of the barn let in a shaft of light, illuminating a long bench with another fly strip dangling above. A vise mounted on the corner told me I had found what I was looking for: Eli's workshop.

Since he hadn't brought the gun to the henhouse, I figured maybe he had it stored in here. If I couldn't find it, I'd have to search for another type of weapon. A hatchet would have been perfect, but I'd settle for a hammer.

I set off in that direction. Three steps in, a cat hissed, causing me to jump. It darted out of my path into the shadows of the barn. I shook my head and released a long exhale, then continued my blind stumble toward the day-lit workshop.

As I approached the workbench, I noticed the galvanized bucket, its broken handle dangling, sitting in the center. Behind it sat my brothers' clothing in a pile, along with their shoes.

Spotting my jackknife nearby, I snatched it, ran my fingers over it for a moment, and slipped it into my pocket.

At the back of the bench were several unlit oil lamps, with a collection of tools hanging behind them. I scanned them from one end to the other.

A dozen screwdrivers of varying lengths poked through a rack spanning between two wall studs. The whisk broom and the giant dustpan Eli had used to sweep up the loose chicken feed hung above them. Beside it, one of those hand-crank drills that works like an eggbeater, like the one hanging in Grandpa's garage. Grandpa had kept his as a knick-knack, but apparently, the Amish still used them.

A few rusting handsaws with carved, wooden handles dangled on a pegboard, along with sets of pliers and C-clamps.

I did a double-take when I discovered a hacksaw. For a moment, I considered using that and the vise to shorten the chain, but decided I couldn't afford to waste that much time.

The gap between the bench and the wall was filled with a collection of shovels, pitchforks, and rakes. What I didn't see was the gun, or any hatchets or hammers. No keys, either. I slapped the workbench in frustration, kicking up a mushroom cloud of dust.

As I turned to leave, my eyes fell on the only item mounted on the adjacent wall: a long pry bar. I lifted it off its hook and gauged its weight. It was almost as long as my arm and solid enough that a good swing would do some serious damage. Two claws had been formed on one end, nowhere near as sharp as a hatchet, but they would do.

I followed the light streaming in from the cracked-open barn door.

Peeking through the opening, I checked to make sure no one was around before I ducked and scampered across the clearing to the henhouse. Even though I moved quietly, the sound of my footsteps was enough to get the chickens clucking.

Holding up near the front of the coop, I cupped my hand behind my ear and listened. When all I heard was birds tweeting, I peered around the corner. Eli remained where I had left him, still alone, with the filthy bottoms of his bare feet facing me.

I snuck along the front of the coop and paused at its doorstep to examine the house. The curtains fluttered in the windows. Sonny was now lying where he had been sitting, but watching me with his head upright.

As I tiptoed past Eli, I half expected he'd suddenly spring to life and clamp a hand around my ankle, like what always happens in the movies. A strong swing of the pry bar would shatter his wrist, so I held my weapon at the ready. Eli never moved, though.

I scrunched low and hurried across the stretch of lawn. As I drew in on the porch, I slowed my pace and watched for movement in the home's shadowy interior. Seeing nothing, I continued on.

Sonny, who still hadn't moved from his spot on the porch, lowered his head when I got close. His tail started wagging, sweeping just above the floor. When I mounted the first step, the tail wag became livelier, thumping against a column. I pressed my finger against my lips, giving him the "shh" sign, but the attention I gave him only made that tail wag faster.

Squatting beside him, I gave him a few pets with my free hand, then brushed his tail over to the other side of the column, where it wouldn't make as much noise.

From there, I climbed onto the porch and began army-crawling across it. The toughest part was holding the chain so it wouldn't drag on the floor. Although I tried not to breathe hard, it felt like I was gasping for air.

To avoid being seen, I approached from beyond the side of the window. My mouth felt dry, and my heart hammered so fast it felt like it might break free from my chest.

When I reached the window, I pressed up against the siding and slowly leaned toward the opening, far enough for one eye to peek in.

It took a moment for my eye to adjust to the darker interior, but I soon made out two forms sitting side by side, not far from the window. I flinched on reflex, but then again... I pushed my head forward once more, far enough for both of my eyes to see inside.

Yes, thank God, it was my brothers. But what were they doing?

Holding my free hand up to shade my eyes from the sunlight, I did a double-take. Their hair had been put in the distinct Amish boy hairstyle. The twins, who had been fighting with Mom to wear the shaggy "broccoli hair" style that teenage boys wore, had allowed their hair to be combed down and trimmed into a so-called "bowl cut."

I put their hairstyle out of my mind and took another look around. They were sitting at a table, each behind an empty plate. Instead of chairs, they sat on a bench, so it looked more like a picnic table. Because I was out in the daylight and the interior was darker, it was hard to see much else. But an old-fashioned black iron stove told me they were in a kitchen area.

Both stared straight ahead, unfocused. Neither moved. Even though I was almost within arm's reach, they didn't look my way.

With no sign of Ungodly, I let out a soft, "Psst."

The twins gave no reaction.

I said it louder. "Psst."

They *had* to have heard me, but they never even blinked.

A steady thumping sound started up behind me. I looked over my shoulder to find Sonny sitting upright, wagging his tail against the porch column. When I craned my neck further to trace his line of sight, I swallowed hard.

Eli was on his knees, holding his head.

My breath went ragged, and time seemed to stand still as Eli turned to face me.

Knowing I had to act quickly, I set the pry bar on the porch floor, grabbed the windowsill, pushed onto my knees, and stuck my head and neck inside. I reached for Xavier, the closer of the two, but even though I stretched, I couldn't quite reach him.

I backed out and turned to check on Eli. He was now crawling, but not toward me. At first, I wondered why he was going to the chicken coop...until I noticed the gun propped against the side—the side I had never thought to look at. It had been there all along!

Understanding how every second counted, I stood, snaked my whole upper body through the window, and leaned in. I almost toppled over, but I caught my balance and grabbed Xavier by the wrist.

An ear-piercing scream followed. Because the howl started the instant I took hold of Xavier, I thought it was him, so I let go on impulse. But movement beyond the kitchen caught my eye, and I soon realized that's where the shriek was coming from.

The ungodly woman-thing raced toward me from the back of the house with her milky yellow eyes fixed on me, her face contorted hideously as she screamed in fury. Two things shocked me: how quickly she moved, and the way her howl sounded like a *chorus* of voices.

As I squirmed backward through the window frame, a gunshot rang out, and I felt a half dozen wasps sting the side of my leg. At the same moment, Sonny yelped. It all happened so fast.

I freed myself from the window and turned toward Eli, who was standing beside the henhouse holding the gun.

Sonny whimpered and began gnawing at a spot on his hindquarters. I looked down at my leg, and when I saw a bunch of red dots blooming from the side of my knee down my calf, I realized I'd been shot. *Buckshot,* I thought. *It's a shotgun.*

Glancing behind me, I saw a crater blasted in the house siding, where much of the shot had hit. He had mostly missed me. And Sonny, too.

Eli leveled the gun and pointed it at me, and I realized I needed to flee without my brothers.

I bolted. The chain was still looped around my neck, with the free end smacking my leg with each step across the porch. I leaped off the opposite side and around the corner, heading for the rear of the house. My leg burned, but not enough to slow me down.

I passed the well I had heard being pumped the day before, and at that instant, I realized I had left the pry bar on the porch. There was no way I could go back, though.

As I ran along the side of the house, Ungodly's relentless chorus of shrieks seemed to rise in volume. The horrible sound of it filled me with dread. It was the sound of rage, echoing through the valley without pausing, as if she never needed to stop for a breath.

After rounding the rear corner of the house, I almost plowed into a small structure. As I circled behind it, I caught a whiff that told me it was their outhouse.

The sweetcorn stand at the back of the garden I had hidden in came into view. I sprinted toward it, but as I crossed the short clearing between the house and the garden, another shot rang out, and I felt new stings, this time, in my shoulder.

I kept going, squeezing between the cornrows. A moment later, I shot out the opposite end before crossing the clearing without another gunshot going off. I crashed through the brush and disappeared into the woods.

The logical escape path would have been down the driveway, but Eli, standing guard near the top of the drive, ruled that option out. I had no choice but to run deeper into this patch of woods, where I had half a chance of staying hidden, fleeing in the opposite direction from which I had come in.

This also meant I had to forget about my phone. Instead, I'd have to find someone to help.

Running past the place where I had been clubbed felt surreal. As I veered along the edge of the clearing, I spotted the blackened patch centered in the circle, filled with rain-soaked ash.

I pushed the horrible memory of what happened there out of my mind, slowing down long enough to look over my shoulder. Eli was nowhere in sight, so I pressed on.

The fire pit made me think of the wolves, which I had last seen here. Without that pry bar, I had no chance of fighting them off. There was no sign of them, though, so I kept running.

Although I was happy to be free, I hated myself for leaving my brothers behind. Even so, the rational part of me understood that on my own, there was little I could do to help them.

That terrible shrieking sound continued, but there was one good thing about it: as I hoofed it through the woods, the volume dropped, telling me she was still back at the house.

The further I ran, the more I thought about how, heading this way, I wouldn't know how to get back to camp. I told myself the most important thing was to avoid being shot, and if I could do that,

I might survive. Yeah, I was in a remote area, but eventually, I *had* to come across someone who could help me.

Soon, I was panting hard, and the pain in my leg and shoulder had worsened. Another backward glance confirmed no one was following me, so I slowed my pace to a jog.

When the upward slope I'd been following leveled off, I concluded I had reached the crest of the valley.

But the further I went, the thicker the woods became. My mind kept going back to the Grimm fairy tale about the poor, starving kids, Hansel and Gretel, who had been hopelessly lost in a dense forest. A white bird led them to a gingerbread house, which turned out to belong to a witch. She took the kids captive, fattening them up to eat.

That was the point where I started thinking of Ungodly as a witch. The idea came from a children's fairy tale, but in my distraught state of mind, it totally fit.

As I continued my slog, I kept checking behind me, but as far as I could see, nobody was following me. The problem was, as thick as the woods had become, I couldn't see far. I told myself that Eli could not have kept up, though, given his age and head injury. I was in rough shape, but he was worse.

After a while, I stopped, cocked my head, and held my labored breathing. I could no longer hear Ungodly howling. Whether she had quit or I was out of earshot, I couldn't say, but I was glad not to have to listen to it anymore. But then, I started wondering if she might be following me in silence, which prompted me to hurry along.

The woods seemed to go on forever. As I trudged through, the pain in my shoulder and leg became almost unbearable. Maybe it was because I was no longer fueled by panic, but it felt like my flesh was tearing where the buckshot had gone in, and I was now wincing with each step.

It got so bad I started considering digging out the shot with the pocketknife, but decided I'd do more harm than good. *Leave it there,* I told myself. *It can't be too much longer.* I had no good reason to believe this, but saying it comforted me anyway.

Sometime later, I spied a clearing up ahead, so I willed myself to continue.

The hopeful sign of civilization must've had me jacked up, because where the woods ended, I damn near walked into a rusty barbed wire fence. I caught myself just in time, saving me from a nasty gash and maybe a case of tetanus.

I was overjoyed to see the top of a barn break the horizon at the far end of a hayfield. Beside it stood one of those steel windmills, like the one in The Wizard of Oz.

But the field was long, so even though it was on a downward slope, crossing it would be a huge challenge.

I inspected my burning leg and shoulder. Blood oozed out of each pockmark, and the entire area had swollen and turned pale. The sight of it made me feel faint. But maybe my lightheadedness was caused by the ever-rising pain. I wanted to lie down and rest, but if I did that, I might not get back up.

Keep going, I told myself. *Your brothers need you.*

I limped along the wire until I found a broken stretch, gave one more look back to confirm no one was heading my way, then stepped into the wet hayfield.

Chapter 15

Between taking more buckshot and having to hold me upright while walking, my leg bothered me more than my shoulder. It kept getting worse, too.

Eventually, I felt like I could no longer bear the pain. I leaned on my knees, grimaced, and sucked air through my teeth.

Looking back, I traced the path I had cut through the hay from the tree line, then switched my gaze to the barn. Although I told myself I was halfway there, deep down inside, I knew it wasn't even close.

But then, for the first time, I spotted what looked like the ridge of a home's roof poking up beside the barn. My spark of hope faded when the memory of those abandoned houses I had passed while chasing the buggy came back to me. If I made it across the field only to discover another deserted house...

Don't think about that, I said to myself. *Just keep going.*

I nodded, channeled my strength, stood upright, and pushed on.

As I dragged myself across the field with that chain draped over my neck, I strained to block out the pain, gluing my eyes on that roof. By the time I was *truly* halfway to the house, I could see it was kept up, not abandoned. Thank God.

Better yet, it was a typical farmhouse, not built in the Amish style. Don't get me wrong: logically, I knew Eli and Ungodly were no ordinary Amish, but my PTSD-impaired brain feared there might be something wrong with *other* Amish people in this area, too. If not that, maybe another Amish household would alert Eli and Ungodly of my whereabouts.

But there was something else, more important: an Amish household wouldn't have a phone, so a quick call for help would be out of the question. There'd be no car either.

The last part of my trek across the field seemed to get more torturous with each step, and before long, I was whimpering out loud and having trouble seeing, with tears blurring my vision. I tried to wipe my eyes and cheeks dry with my fists, but more kept coming.

I felt as though I was about to collapse. Actually, the idea sounded better than staying on my feet. I was like a sputtering car, out of gas, running on fumes.

I tried to focus on the farm's details. A neat vegetable garden sat between the hayfield and the barn. An antique pickup truck was the only vehicle in sight, parked in the driveway with its rear end facing me and its hood open. Although the truck was caked in dirt, I could see enough of the paint to tell it was blue, with white lettering across the tailgate spelling out STUDEBAKER.

All that dirt struck me as wrong. My grandpa had a '67 Pontiac GTO, his pride and joy. Dad shared that love with him. Until Dad got sick, the two of them would constantly wash and wax "the Goat," as GTOs were called, so it always looked bright and shiny. I figured anyone with an antique car would do the same, so why would this owner let their Studebaker get so dirty?

When I was a stone's throw from the end of the hayfield, a dog's bark startled me. Then I saw the beast streaking out from the barn's shadows. There was no leash holding it back.

I stopped in my tracks and went rigid, too worn out to retreat. Within seconds, two more barking dogs were bearing down on me from other parts of the yard. *If only I had that pry bar* flashed through my mind. I pulled the knife out of my pocket, opened it, and grasped it by the handle.

The dogs converged at the end of the driveway but stopped there. They lined up in a row, like guards standing in formation, barking ferociously as a pack. I stayed where I was, which seemed to hold them at bay. For now.

Standing still made me feel even woozier, though. Fighting to stay upright, I tried to lock my knees, but the leg with the buckshot was too swollen. I took deep breaths and prayed for the strength to stay on my feet, afraid that if I went down, the dogs would see me as vulnerable and attack.

A loud, shrill whistle sounded. The dogs snapped into growls while holding their collective glare on me.

Movement at the home's rear door caught my attention. An old man wearing blue jean overalls slid out through the screen door, which slammed behind him, as Eli's had.

At first, I was happy to see him, but then I noticed he was carrying a gun, and that feeling withered. I groaned when he leveled it at me, and I asked myself, *Sure, you escaped, but to what?*

A minute ago, I thought I was in the clear because this wasn't an Amish farm, but what if something's wrong with this *whole area?*

While raising my hands in surrender, my thoughts shifted. I must have looked like hell, all torn up, dirty, bloody, shackled at the waist, with a chain draped around my neck. And what was I holding? A knife. The sight of me would've alarmed anyone in their right mind.

I wanted to yell out, *No, you've got it all wrong. I'm a victim, not a threat.* But it took all my effort just to stay upright, so I said nothing.

I could barely lift my wounded arm, so the best I could do was stick my hands out. I thought about dropping the knife, but it was my only defense. Instead, I tried to hold it so it wouldn't be so obvious and avoided pointing the knife at the man, hoping that if he did see it, it wouldn't look as threatening.

"What do you want?" he yelled.

"I need help." I tried to yell my response, but as weak as I felt, I barely got it out.

"Who are you?"

His question confused me. He probably wasn't asking for my name. Most likely, he wanted to know why I showed up out of nowhere, looking like something out of a horror movie. But where would I start?

I tried blurting out my name, but my throat felt strangled. The world began to spin.

My legs gave out, and the last thing I saw was the hayfield coming up to meet me.

Chapter 16

THE NEXT THING I knew, a dog had bitten into my shoulder. I tried to roll away, but it clenched harder, digging its teeth deeper into my muscle, sending white-hot pain through my entire arm.

I squeezed the knife with my other hand, getting ready to stab the animal with it. But a few hazy seconds later, my brain registered that my hand was empty.

All I could do was punch the dog with my empty fist. One swat, and my knuckles glanced off something too thin and bony to be a dog. Another hand grabbed mine and clamped it. "Whoa there, Missy."

I peeled open my eyes, blinking against the bright daylight, then turned toward the voice.

The old man was sitting beside me, wearing a pair of glasses with round lenses wrapped in wire rims. He slowly let go of my hand, patted it gently, then leaned back and moved the glasses onto his head.

That's when I noticed a pair of bloody tweezers between his thumb and forefinger in his other hand. He must've seen me staring at it, because he raised his eyebrows and said, "We gotta get this buckshot out of there."

I looked around and discovered I was in a house, lying on a couch in a living room. My boots were not on my feet. He must've carried me here...to this makeshift operating room.

I asked, "How long was I out?" My voice sounded thin and raspy.

He looked at his watch and scratched his chin. "Maybe two hours?"

Wow, I thought. *I guess I* was *running on fumes.*

I scanned the room. An antique-looking armchair sat across from me with doilies covering the armrests and a bigger one draped over the back. A carved wooden table sat beside the chair, and a small bookshelf was built into the wall behind it, filled with books and magazines.

If there was ever a house that looked like an old person's, this was it.

But as I looked over the lacy curtains covering the window, it dawned on me that this wasn't just an old person's house. It was finished with a woman's touch.

So, where was the woman?

I turned to look at the man. He was examining my shoulder with his nose scrunched up. "Does it hurt?"

I didn't answer, but I thought, *What do you think?*

"Yup," he said, as if the look on my face said it all. "You'll be fine, but it ain't gonna feel like you're picking daisies, now that you're awake."

He dropped the tweezers in a bowl and wiped his hands on a dingy dishrag. "I'll get something for the hurt."

As he moved the bowl to the floor, I heard little pellets rolling around.

"I got six of them bastards," he said, and he smiled at me proudly with perfect white teeth.

Not teeth, I corrected myself, *dentures.*

He rose. "A couple more to go on your arm. It's all swollen up, so I gotta dig a little deeper."

I touched my shoulder and winced. It had mushroomed out like an overfilled water balloon. The achiness had spread all the way down my arm and throughout that side of my torso.

"There's twice as many in your leg."

"I need a hospital," I said. "And the sheriff."

The man blew out a long breath and rubbed the back of his head. "You came at the wrong time for that, Missy. My truck ain't running."

I shot him a look, wondering if that was the truth. But then I remembered the Studebaker with the raised hood. I said, "We can call for help."

He shook his head. "I'm still waiting for phone service here."

You've got to be kidding me, I thought, staring at him. "And you don't have a cell phone?"

He gave me a blank expression. "I got no phone."

I figured maybe he was too old for a cell phone. Like my great-grandmother, who wanted nothing to do with such newfangled things. *Her* word, not mine. Plus, with nothing else around, this might be a coverage dead spot.

"You know, I'm still waiting for power, too. It's been almost twenty years since the REA."

I had no idea what he was talking about, but I noticed an oil lamp sitting on the table, and it sank in. *Unbelievable,* I thought. *This man is living with no phone and no electricity, like the Amish.*

I pushed the thought aside. "We can get help from a neighbor."

He shook his head. "Not in Forgotten Valley. This here valley used to be an Amish settlement. Me and them. But they all picked up and left. Just Eli and Bertha Yoder in these parts now."

Hearing Eli's name made me wince. But now I knew this guy knew of him.

Then, I thought about that name: Bertha. What a horrible name. It fit.

The man was studying me. "That's who shot you, right?"

My throat tightened. "Yeah. My brothers are still there."

He frowned. "Let me guess. They're twins?"

My heart skipped a beat. Nodding slowly, I narrowed my eyes and tried to read his face. What exactly did this man know?

"Identical, right?"

My chest iced over. "How did you know?"

The old man sighed. "That's a long story. We'll get to it."

I fought off the urge to press him on the matter and redirected my focus to the most important thing. "Can we get your truck running?"

"I'm working on that. The doggone carburetor got all gummed up. It's in fifty pieces in my barn." He put his hand against his cheek and shook his head. "Holy Moly, carbs are a lot more complicated than they used to be. Even if all those tiny parts go back together alright, I reckon it'll still take me a day or two to get her running."

I thought of the time Dad and I helped Grandpa rebuild the carburetor on his Goat. I learned first-hand how intricate they were. Dad explained to me how that part was the Achilles' heel of antique cars. They were always causing problems until fuel injection made them obsolete. "And just like that..." Dad had said, snapping his fingers, "...the world became a better place."

"So, your only car is that antique Studebaker?" I asked.

The old man tilted his head and gave me a funny look, like maybe he was a bit offended. "Yeah, all I got is Trotter."

I had to think about what he said for a while before I realized he'd given the truck a nickname.

"But she ain't that old."

I thought, *maybe not for an old-timer like you*. I kept that to myself, though.

"Can I walk to the hospital?"

The man scoffed. "Tri-County Hospital is twenty miles away. I doubt you could even stand for five minutes."

I wanted to argue, but I had little doubt he was right. How I'd made it across that hayfield was a miracle.

"Plus, you don't need a hospital. I can get this shot out myself."

"But my head," I said, reaching up to touch it.

"Let me take a gander."

I lifted my head off the pillow he had propped me against and turned away to give him a good look.

"Mm-hm. I'd say you got your bell rung there."

As I lowered my head, I said, "I need stitches."

He pursed his lips. "It's already scabbing over."

"But without stitches, I'll have a bigger scar."

He held his hands up in the "so what?" motion. "Your hair will cover it. Just be glad you ain't me." He tilted forward to show me his thin head of hair and then grinned.

Still feeling some of the lingering fogginess from the concussion, I gave up on the debate.

"Say, what's your name, Missy?"

"Emma Griffiths."

He leaned over and took my right hand, squeezing it with his heavily calloused fingers and palms. "Pleased to meet you, Emma Griffiths. I'm Clarence John Henry. Clarence, for short."

His gesture put me at ease. I squeezed his hand back.

Before I had a chance to say anything, he released me, saying, "Let me get you something for the hurt." He turned and wandered away.

I tried to sit up, but even that felt like a chore. It was like everything that had happened had caught up with me. My mind felt drained, and my body was spent.

I had no choice but to put my faith in Clarence. Was that a good idea?

Clattering sounds came from the nearby room. "Where's your wife?" I called.

The noise stopped. "Bessie passed on. Three years ago. Consumption got her."

"I'm sorry," I said, half wondering what consumption was. It sounded vaguely familiar, but I decided he must be using an old-fashioned word.

"Much obliged." The clattering started again. "It gets lonely here since she left. We never had kids. Wanted 'em, but I guess none of 'em wanted us back."

I heard footsteps and saw movement in the corner of my eye as Clarence returned to the room.

"We're in business." He held a jar in one hand and two small glasses in the other, with his pointer finger wrapped around a wooden spoon. Tucked under his arm, a corked bottle. He gave the jar a shake, rattling it. "Morphine. Left over from Bessie's last days."

"Morphine?" All I could think of was the Civil War.

Clarence held out the wooden spoon. "And you can bite on this."

Oh, my God, I thought. This *is* like the Civil War.

"I'll give you a swig or three of my moonshine, too." He sat on the chair and held out the bottle. "Finest hooch in Homer County."

I wouldn't have minded doing a shot. I did my share of them at parties. But grown-ups weren't serving them. "I'm only eighteen," I said.

"Well, you're old enough for three-two beer, so I'd say you're close enough."

Three-two beer. I rolled the words over until I uncovered a half-forgotten memory of Mom explaining how they used to sell lower alcohol beer in Ohio, limited to 3.2% alcohol. Back in the day, you only had to be eighteen to drink it. Apparently, Clarence thought this was still a thing.

He poured the moonshine into the two glasses and handed me one. Holding out his own in a toasting gesture, he said, "Bottom's up," and downed it. I watched him as he sucked a breath through his dentures.

"What?" he asked. "You reckon I *want* to be doing this?" He pointed at my shoulder with his chin.

I shrugged.

"No way, Missy. Doing this while dressing a deer back in my hunting days was one thing. But doing this to a person?" He shook his head, poured himself another shot and downed it, then nodded at my glass. "Take a swig now, but save some to wash down the painkillers."

I took a sip of the moonshine, which had a strong, sharp taste that made my eyes water.

Clarence smiled, then picked up the jar, opened it, and shook out two pills. "The doc said Bessie should take one pill at a time, but if things got bad, she could take two." He handed me two pills.

When I reluctantly took them, he must have sensed my hesitation, because he said, "I have aspirin, too, if you prefer that. He looked down at my leg and scratched his head. "I reckon that won't do the trick, though."

He was probably right. And with no way to get immediate help, I knew I had to get the buckshot out of me.

Deciding I had little choice in the matter, I shoved the pills into my mouth. They stuck to my tongue, so I had to roll them free. I took a sip of the hooch and swallowed, but the pills lodged in my burning throat. I took a mouthful to wash them down, but that got me coughing.

I'm not sure why Clarence didn't offer me a glass of water—or why I didn't ask for one, for that matter. I didn't want to be a wimp about it, but swallowing those pills with that moonshine made me feel like I was being choked. I reminded myself that compared to all the awful things I'd been through, this was nothing.

"Bet you feel better without that shackle," Clarence said.

I moved my hand down to my waist, but couldn't find the belt. For the first time, I realized I was lying flat on my back, which wouldn't have been possible if the padlock had been there. "Where did it go?"

Clarence dug something out of his overalls' bib pocket. He held up a bobby pin and flashed a smug smile. "Courtesy of Bessie."

"You picked the lock?"

"Sure did. That antique was simple as pie. Old contraptions like that are the easiest to pick."

"Huh. Thank you." Although nothing had changed, I felt better knowing I no longer had that thing attached. Then again, maybe the alcohol played a role, because I was feeling warm and tingly, and a bit off-balance.

Clarence waved off my thanks. "While we wait for that morphine to kick in, are you hungry? I picked my first batch of peaches this morning."

"Yes, please." It wasn't just my hunger. He was offering my favorite fruit. "You grow peaches?"

He looked at me funny and pushed up from the chair. "Sure do."

I had always thought peaches came from the south—like Georgia, but I guess people who live in the country grow just about anything.

A minute later, Clarence was back. He handed me one peach and chomped down on another. When juice dribbled down his chin, he slurped on the peach and wiped his face on the short sleeve of his T-shirt.

I looked my peach over. It was small and covered with blemishes, but when I bit into it, it was sweet and full of flavor. I took nibbles, hoping to avoid spilling juice down my chin, since he hadn't offered me a napkin.

"This might be the most delicious peach I've ever eaten," I said between bites. I didn't mention how ugly it was, but I meant it—even though hunger might have affected my judgment.

"This hot, sunny summer is perfect for peaches. Not so good for my apple tree, though."

I didn't argue with him about the weather, although I knew we had an unusual number of cool, cloudy days, having worked as a lifeguard. Of course, the local weather might've differed from Cleveland Heights, which was affected by Lake Erie.

Clarence finished his peach before I finished mine. Without even asking if I wanted another, he went back to the kitchen and came back with four more.

By the time I had finished my third peach, I could tell the morphine was kicking in, bringing my first feeling of calm since all the craziness had begun. I was even stressing less about my brothers, although nothing had changed, so it was clearly the drugs making me think about them more distantly.

"Are you ready?" Clarence asked, as if he had sensed my mood shift.

I shrugged. "Are you as good at surgery as you are at growing peaches?"

"I ain't hunted since I was a boy, but in those days, I was the best at getting buckshot out. It's the same idea, I reckon."

"Then, let's go." I still wasn't certain I should trust this stranger, but I needed to get it over with; what choice did I have, anyway? "I'm as ready as I'm going to be."

"Dandy. Let's get cracking." Clarence held up the wooden spoon.

I scoffed at it and shook my head.

He set the bowl on the edge of the couch, drizzled some moonshine over the tweezers, slid his glasses down from his head onto his nose, and leaned closer to my shoulder.

Here we go, Doctor Clarence, I thought. It had to have been the morphine that made calling him that seem funny rather than troubling.

But even in my drugged-out mind, I knew this was no laughing matter.

Chapter 17

I stared at the ceiling while Dr. Clarence went to work on my shoulder. When I felt the tweezers stabbing into my flesh, I realized that although the morphine had dulled the pain, it couldn't totally negate the dreadfulness of what was happening.

All I could do was squeeze my eyes shut and endure. I reminded myself that I'd made it through the chicken coop ordeal, so I could make it through this.

"Hold still," Clarence said, sounding a bit irritated.

I thought I was, but apparently, I'd been squirming.

With the help of the morphine, it was mostly pressure that I felt. I'd call it discomfort, but not really pain. The worst part was thinking about what Clarence was doing and the sickening sensation of the tweezers rooting around inside me.

"Where're you hiding, you little bugger?"

I winced as he dug deeper.

"There you are, bastard."

I literally felt Clarence extract the piece of shot, dragging it out through the hole in my skin, leaving me nauseous.

"Wanna see?"

I didn't, but I unpeeled my eyes. He held it up proudly, like he'd unearthed a little treasure. It looked like a bloody ball bearing. When he dropped it into the bowl, it made a pinging sound. "One more, then I'm on to the leg."

He didn't bother showing me the last one. When I heard it ping, he said, "You're doing great, Missy."

He repositioned his chair beside my leg. "Keep up the good work."

I felt like I should offer a compliment in return. That would be the polite thing to do. But the truth was, I had no idea if he was doing a good job or if he was a total hack, so I kept quiet.

As he worked the tweezers into the next hole, I sucked a breath through my teeth.

"That hurt?" he asked.

I rocked my hand in the "so-so" gesture. "Might be more tender down there from walking on it."

"Could be," Clarence said. "Need another shot of hooch?"

I shook my head. "But maybe that wooden spoon isn't such a dumb idea."

He chuckled and handed it to me. I slipped the spoon across my mouth but held off on clamping down.

Clarence began humming that "Swanee River" song. When I felt the tweezers burrow into my flesh, I clenched down, sinking my teeth into the wood.

The tweezers ground through the meat of my calf as Clarence searched for the piece of shot. He stopped his tune to say, "Here we go," yanking it out through the cut.

The ball pinged when he dropped it into the bowl. "I'm working from the bottom up."

I thought it might be best if he didn't give me a blow-by-blow account, so I said nothing, figuring if I responded, I'd be encouraging him.

I had to find a way to quit thinking about what he was doing. I came up with the idea of using mind over matter to disconnect circuits in my nervous system, blocking sensations in my legs. Being high, this seemed entirely plausible. Maybe it *was* possible, because it seemed to help. Or maybe the morphine was now working at full effect. I was lucky he had them on hand.

When Clarence started humming again, he switched to "I've Been Working on the Railroad." I followed along, but with my mouth locked onto the spoon, all I could do was voice the lyrics inside my head:

> I've been workin' on the railroad,
> All the live long day.
> I've been workin' on the railroad,
> Just to pass the time away.

I couldn't remember what came next, so I hummed silently along until he got to the chorus:

> Dinah, won't you blow,
> Dinah, won't you blow,
> Dinah, won't you blow your horn, your horn?
> Dinah, won't you blow,
> Dinah, won't you blow,
> Dinah, won't you blow your horn?

The chorus took me back to when I was younger. We had a cat named Dinah, who might have been the meanest cat that ever lived.

She especially hated Dad, even though he was always kind to her. Every time he'd walk by, she'd hiss and swipe at him with her claws.

I barely noticed the next ping or two.

The tune "On Top of Old Smokey" came next. Inside my head, I followed along using the parody lyrics we sang as kids, since that's all I could remember:

On top of spaghetti
All covered with cheese
I lost my poor meatball
When somebody sneezed.
It rolled off the table
And onto the floor
And then my poor meatball
Rolled out of the door.

I couldn't recall the rest, so I just repeated those two verses.

"Oh! Susanna" came next on the playlist, which I started humming out loud. "Yankee Doodle" followed, then "Billy Boy" and "Down in the Valley."

I was all wrapped up in the songs and had half forgotten about what Clarence was doing by the time he announced, "All done, Missy." The last piece pinged in the bowl, followed by the clatter of the tweezers.

My leg throbbed with a dull ache, but at the moment, I didn't care. I wished we could have kept on humming, but Clarence must've read my mind, because he said, "Just in time, too. I ran out of old tunes, and I don't know any new ones."

I laughed. "No surprise there, seeing as you have no electricity."

Clarence splashed moonshine on my leg, making it sting. He fanned it with his hand. "I got no bandages, either," he said.

I lifted my head and leaned forward to look. My leg was pale and puffed up, and the nasty wounds looked like wormholes. "They're not really bleeding, right?"

"Nope. You'll be alright without bandages."

He said it so reassuringly, I had to remind myself he knew nothing about healthcare.

"So, how did you know my brothers are twins?" My question spilled out without me even thinking about it.

Clarence sat back, sighed, and folded his arms. "That's a long story. Let's talk about that after the morphine wears off. For now, are you up for a meal?"

The idea of sitting down for lunch struck me as absurd. I hadn't seen my brothers in hours. I didn't know what was going on with them, and I wasn't out rescuing them. But this guy thinks I should sit down and eat?

Some rational part of my brain told me to give it a rest. Sure, the sooner I heard what Clarence knew, the sooner I might get to the bottom of things. Except something told me I'd need to be thinking clearly for that discussion.

And, oh yeah...having just gone through a living room surgery and still being under the influence of opioids, I wasn't exactly in superhero condition. Getting some food in me would do me some good. "What's to eat?"

"I smoked a nice ham last week."

I tried to picture what that meant. Like, how do you do that? "You *smoked* it?"

He gave me a questioning look. "Sure did. Preserves the meat. I got no icebox."

I almost laughed about how he called it an icebox instead of a refrigerator. "Right. No electricity. Where did you get the ham?"

He pointed out back. "My hog pen's next to the barn."

I wiped my hand down my face, feeling like I had stepped back in time.

Without warning, Clarence poured moonshine over my shoulder. I grimaced at the burn, but it was more from the surprise than anything.

"Sorry 'bout that. Gotta disinfect it, even though I hate wasting the hooch!" He fanned my shoulder for a few seconds, then started gathering the items he'd used for the operation. "Do you reckon you can get up if I help you?"

I lifted my head. "I think so." Maybe it was my imagination, but my wounds felt better now that they were free of buckshot. Or that could be the painkillers talking.

Clarence looked at me doubtfully. "Maybe you should rest."

I shook my head. Although I wasn't entirely convinced I could stand, I had to try. I couldn't remember why, but I knew hospitals made patients move as soon as possible after surgery.

Plus, my best chance to get back on my feet was before the morphine wore off. I had no complaints about the feeling they'd given me, but I had no plans to take more. And anyway, I couldn't rest until I got my brothers away from Ungodly.

"Let me put this stuff away, then I'll help you up." He headed off to the kitchen.

I grabbed the back of the couch with my good arm, swung my feet off onto the floor, and dragged myself upright. Moving gave me discomfort in my arm and leg, but I was determined to gut through it. A wave of dizziness followed, though, so I stayed put until Clarence returned.

"You're halfway there," he said when he saw me sitting up, and he flashed me a denture-grin of encouragement.

He stood in front of me, planting his feet shoulder-width apart, and held out both hands. As I grasped his calloused fingers and pulled, he leaned back to counterbalance my weight and lugged me upright.

I stood on wobbly legs, not letting go of him as I worked to steady myself. It hadn't been long since I ran away from Eli and Ungodly—Bertha, I mean—but in that short time, I had turned into a cripple.

Eventually, Clarence shuffled clear to give me some room. He studied my face. "You okay?"

I nodded.

Not fully trusting me, Clarence circled to my side with his hands at the ready. I took a baby step, then another, and soon I was heading for the kitchen. "Take a seat at the table," Clarence said, and he hurried in front of me to pull out the chair.

Proud of myself for having made the walk on my own power, I slid into the seat and scanned the room. I already knew there wouldn't be a refrigerator, but the sight of a black cast-iron wood-burning stove—like the one in Ungodly's kitchen—surprised me.

"Want a glass of water?"

As soon as he said it, I realized how dry my mouth felt. I hadn't peed since the morning, and still didn't need to. Maybe part of my problem was dehydration. Maybe a lot of it. "That sounds great."

Clarence removed two glasses from the cupboard and poured water from a pitcher on the counter. The pitcher was depression glass, much like the one Eli had given me, except this one was pink.

He handed me one of the glasses and took a long guzzle from the other.

I sipped the water, pausing to assess the taste. It tasted good, without the mineral taste of Eli's well water. Still, I knew I should pace myself. I took another swig. "You don't have well water?"

"We have a spring here." He pointed through the window at a small building behind the house, up the hill.

I studied it. "Is that an outhouse?"

Clarence chuckled. "That there's the springhouse, where our water comes from. It's cooler in there than the cellar, so that's where I store food in the summer. Please don't use it as an outhouse!" He laughed again.

I giggled along while giving him the okay sign.

He opened a door in the side of the stove and peered inside. "There's still embers in here, so it'll be ready in a jiffy." He began feeding it fresh sticks from a bucket on the floor, which soon burst into flames. He closed the door and adjusted some vent dials. "Will you be alright here while I head out back?"

After giving him a nod, I took another gulp of water.

"Need a refill?"

I looked at my glass, which was now half empty. "I can get it."

He knitted his brow and watched me for a spell before turning and leaving through the back door, carrying a canvas bag. The screen door slammed behind him.

A few more swigs, and the water was gone, so I pushed up from the chair and shambled over to the counter. I felt weak, but steady enough to walk, which gave me confidence.

I watched Clarence disappear into the springhouse through the window over the sink. The dogs, which had followed him there, sat waiting for him outside the door.

I poured more water from the pink pitcher and raised the glass to my lips. As I sipped, I examined the advertising calendar pinned to the side of the cupboard:

Butler Feed Mill

Serving Homer County since 1883

Suddenly, something struck me as wrong. Feeling like my knees were turning to jelly, I grabbed hold of the counter to brace myself and thought, *Wait...what?*

The year on the calendar read "1955."

I stopped breathing while my mind spun into a frenzy, skittering through a series of subconscious observations I had made. No electricity. No phone. That blank stare Clarence gave me when I mentioned a cell phone. A house filled with antiques. I looked out the window at that old pickup truck, which he said wasn't old.

The screen door clattered, snatching me out of my rising spiral of panic. Clarence pushed in, carrying the now-full canvas bag. He stopped and gave me a concerned look.

I had probably turned as white as snow.

"You alright, Missy?"

Unable to answer, I sucked in a hissing breath. My head swirled, and stomach acid burned the back of my throat. I slurped down some water, fighting to pull myself together.

"Clarence..." Pressing my hand against my forehead, I had to stop for another gasp of air. "...what year is it?"

He pulled back his head and gave me a long, questioning look while chewing his lower lip, as if trying to gauge whether he'd given me too much morphine.

After a while, he cleared his throat and said, "It's 1955."

Chapter 18

Maybe it was the cumulative effect of all the nightmarish things I'd been through, but this gut punch just about did me in.

I sat in the living room armchair with my face buried in my hands and my brain churning, trying desperately to make sense of it all.

As frazzled as I felt at that moment, I wondered how I would've handled it without the soothing effect of the morphine. I would have lost it, for sure.

With my stomach doing somersaults, I distractedly flipped through the pieces of Clarence's mail and the newspaper in my lap one more time. The postmarks and the Homer Reporter's front-page date were all marked "1955," and none of them showed any yellowing from age.

The most indisputable evidence of all was his driver's license, a piece of paper labeled "1954 Operator's License," with the name Clarence J. Henry and the birthdate 07-19-75 typed in the fields. *1875,* I thought in bewilderment. It all proved clearly that Clarence wasn't senile—because at first, that's what I had assumed.

He worked silently in the kitchen, leaving me alone to come to grips with what I'd learned, knowing he had no answers to offer me.

I took a deep breath and told myself to stay calm and think, then went back to paging through my recollections, searching for an answer to the first question: when did time change?

The Amish shun technology, so they live in 2025 virtually the same way they would've lived in 1955. The same way they would've lived in 1895, for that matter. Thinking back on everything that happened at that farm, I couldn't pinpoint anything that would tell me it was 2025. But at the time, there was nothing strange about this.

The wooden bucket had struck me as odd, though. I had wondered if they still made them, but I soon forgot all about it. There was no way something like that would survive a century of usage. Now I realize that thing probably wasn't as ancient as I had thought.

But the tools in the barn were a different story. Yeah, they all looked old. Tools were built to last, though. Some of Dad's tools came from his grandfather. So, the Amish were probably using many ancient tools, even in 2025.

I thought about the padlock that Clarence had picked. He had said it was old. Old was right, including for someone with a 1955 perspective.

The gun. Now, it was coming back to me. Even to me, not exactly a firearms expert, that thing looked ancient. I had pegged it as a World War I artifact. But if that were the case, in 1955, it wouldn't have been considered particularly old.

Putting it all together now, chances were, it was 1955 the whole time I was at the Yoder farm.

With my mind reeling with this realization, I barely noticed when Clarence came to get me. "Are you up to eating?"

His question jarred me out of my manic state. With him standing at the edge of the living room, our eyes met, and I spotted the look of worry in his, like he wanted to help me, but didn't know how.

I realized then how confused he must have been after a battered girl showed up and announced that she came from seventy years in the future. What must *he* be thinking?

Amazingly, he had shown zero doubt about my claim that I came from 2025. At least, if he didn't believe me, he never let on. He could have easily concluded I was having a morphine-induced delusion, but he never questioned it. Looking back now, I think this man was used to dealing with unexplainable things.

I wiped my hands down my face and blew out a long exhale. "I can't believe it, Clarence. I'm thinking the whole time I was at the Yoder farm, it was 1955."

He rubbed the back of his head. "So, when did the year change?"

I pressed both fists against my mouth and squeezed my eyes shut, racking my brain. "I don't know," I muttered slowly, scrolling through the sequence of events from that night.

Then, it registered. At first, I almost glossed over it, but my mind latched onto something and reeled back to it.

"Wait," I said, dredging up a half-forgotten memory. "The pond!"

I strained to reformulate what happened and play it back. "After I dove in and resurfaced, the duckweed was gone."

"Duckweed?"

"Yeah. It made no sense, but with everything I was dealing with, I never gave it a second thought. Until now."

Clarence said nothing, like he wasn't really following this.

"There was something else, too. I saw a purple mist draped over the surface when I came up for air. It hadn't been there before I went under."

"Purple?" He arched an eyebrow at me.

I didn't bother to explain it. I couldn't explain it. But I knew it meant something.

"And then there's the question of why Bertha took my brothers into the pond in the first place. At the time, I believed she was going to drown them, but she took them in one side and out the other."

"So, what was the point of that?"

"Exactly. Because it wasn't just a pond. She turned it into some sort of weird time-travel wormhole."

"Huh?"

I learned the term "wormhole" in my honors physics class, but I let it go. I spelled it out as clearly as I could. "Ungodly used the pond as a time portal. Before we went under, it was 2025. When we resurfaced, it was 1955."

I rested my elbow on the chair's arm and pressed my forehead into my palm. "After I went into the pond, I had no reason to look back at the tents, so I didn't bother. But if I had..."

"They would have been gone," Clarence finished for me.

I pointed at him. "You nailed it."

It was a dumbfounding concept, and it hit me like a blow to the head.

I felt my heart sink as a new realization dawned on me. Even if I *could* get back to my phone in the year I came from, it would do me no good. Because how could the sheriff rescue my brothers when they were stuck in a different era, seventy years earlier?

The infuriating truth was that getting my phone back would be pointless.

My head buzzed like a hornet's nest with other unanswerable questions. How would I navigate getting help in a different year—in an era I didn't understand? Even if I could rescue my brothers, would we be stuck in a whole new world? Or could we get back to the time we belong in simply by reversing course through the pond?

I couldn't wrap my mind around what it all meant.

"Let's eat," Clarence said. "It'll do you some good."

I sucked in a deep inhale, then gave my head a quick shake as if to clear out the chaos. "You're probably right about that, although I'm not exactly hungry."

I gathered the pile of papers and held it out to him. He tucked it under his arm and stood nearby as I pushed myself up from the chair. As I straightened, I only vaguely noticed the throbbing in my leg and arm.

Clarence cautiously watched me cross the room, prepared to give me a hand if needed, tracking me into the kitchen. "After we eat, I'll get to work on that carburetor. While I do that, you should get a nap before the soreness returns."

I stopped and frowned. "You said we'd talk."

Clarence walked around me and headed for the table. "Oh, we'll be talking. But I've gotta get Trotter running. And you need rest. Can we wait till tonight?"

He said it like a question, but he wasn't expecting an answer. Yeah, I needed to rest, but there was no way I could relax with the twins under Ungodly's spell. I couldn't argue about the Trotter part, though. The sooner that truck was running, the better. I slumped my shoulders, nodded, and followed him to the table.

"I could use a shower, too," I added, suddenly thinking this might help ease me out of my crazed state of mind.

Clarence pulled my chair out for me. "You're in luck. We added an indoor bathroom with a tub and shower about twenty-five years ago."

Although I hadn't considered that he might not have indoor plumbing, I was glad to hear he did. I did the math. It was 1930 when the house got indoor plumbing. "I bet Bessie was thrilled."

"Over the moon, I'd say. She'd been asking for it since moving in. This was my parents' house before us."

As I slid into my seat, I finally noticed the spread of food in the center of the table. It seemed like there was enough to feed four. "This looks delicious."

He waved it off, took the seat across from me, and gestured to the serving plates. "Eat up. It'll help you heal."

I stabbed the serving fork into a slice of ham.

"It's gonna take us some time to trade stories," Clarence said, spooning some fried potatoes and zucchini onto his plate. "Hopefully, you'll be up for it."

"I'll be up for it," I said without hesitation. It was going to be hard enough to wait until evening.

"The morphine will wear off before then," he pointed out.

"I'll be up for it," I repeated.

Chapter 19

I leaned on the banister as I worked my way down the stairway, wincing with each step. The painkillers had worn off hours ago, but Clarence had given me the aspirin bottle. Once the aspirin kicked in, the pain seemed more tolerable.

Or, who knows? Maybe my mind was too preoccupied with finding a way out of this living nightmare. I had waited long enough to hear what Clarence knew, and I was *so* ready for this moment.

As I approached the bottom of the stairway, I vaguely noticed a pleasing smell, but I didn't pay enough attention to recognize it consciously.

Clarence looked up when I turned into the living room. I should call it the parlor, because that's what he called it.

Wearing Bessie's clothes made me feel *really* weird. After my long nap, but before my shower, he had shown me her closet and dresser, still packed with her belongings. "Help yourself to anything you'd like," he said with a sniffle.

After going through it all, I almost decided to put my own clothes back on. But those were disgusting, and since I had showered, I told myself I'd have to wait until I could give them a good wash. I even considered asking Clarence for a pair of his pants. But something told me all he had were overalls, and I'd be swimming in them.

I eventually picked one of Bessie's nightgowns and covered that up with her bathrobe. Although I felt a little freaky dressed in this costume, it was sure nice to be wearing something clean.

I drew the line at Bessie's old granny panties, though. Before I could reflexively shut that drawer, what I saw was frumpier than I ever thought possible. Even if that weren't the case, the idea of wearing someone else's underwear turned my stomach. I went commando instead, figuring I was safe with the nightgown and bathrobe both reaching my ankles.

So, here I was, making my grand entrance, dressed like Bessie.

Sitting on the couch, Clarence did a double-take. "You're roughly the same size," he said, then he fidgeted and averted his gaze, which made me feel a bit less creeped out.

Thankfully, he changed the subject promptly. "How was the shower?"

I gave him a thumbs-up as I headed to the doily-covered armchair. The truth was, it was the weakest shower I'd ever taken. The water came from a cistern, filled by a pump powered by that Wizard of Oz windmill. When Clarence explained the setup to me, I was glad that all we had to do was tap into city water.

Anyway, that's the reason for the low water pressure. Even so, it might've qualified for the most wonderful shower I'd ever taken.

I lowered myself into the seat while trying to avoid bending my injured leg any more than I had to.

Clarence leaned over and grabbed two bowls from the end table beside the couch. He motioned to the table beside my armchair. "I made us my favorite evening snacks."

Two bowls sat beside the unlit oil lamp. When I saw popcorn in the first, that's when I put a finger on that pleasant smell I had half-noticed while coming down the steps. Since he didn't have a microwave, my mind went to Jiffy Pop. "You made popcorn?"

He looked at me funny and nodded slowly. "Freshly popped in bacon grease. The best way." He raised the other bowl. "Fresh blackberries, too."

I looked at the second bowl, filled with plump blackberries, sugar sprinkled over them, and my mouth watered. "Yum," I said.

"And a glass of Ovaltine."

I almost laughed when I heard that word. I never tried it. But it was part of the movie *A Christmas Story,* and my grandpa had told me how his mom would serve Ovaltine as a treat when he was growing up. Hiding my smile, I thanked him, picked up the glass, took a sniff, then a sip.

It was actually pretty good. Tasted like a malt milkshake, except not cold. Since I probably still needed to catch up on hydration, I gulped down half of the glass before I wondered how old this springhouse-stored milk might be. If the thought had occurred to me sooner, I might have skipped the Ovaltine.

Clarence popped a blackberry into his mouth. He wiped his fingertips on the thigh of his overalls, leaving two purple smudges.

I followed his cue and tried a blackberry, which turned out to be the sweetest, most flavorful berry I'd ever had. It left behind drops of purple juice on my fingertips. Since he hadn't given me a napkin, and since I wasn't going to wipe them on Bessie's bathrobe, I decided I'd have to let it air dry.

"I'm almost done reassembling the carb," Clarence said. "If all goes well, Trotter will be running tomorrow afternoon."

Antsy for running transportation, I asked, "Can we get it going in the morning?"

He shook his head. "I need another hour or two before I can even mount it. Gotta tend to the morning chores first."

I didn't understand what was so pressing. Although I felt bad, I couldn't resist pushing the matter. "Can the chores wait?"

Clarence squirmed in his seat. "I'll put off what I can. But the animals have to be watered and fed, their bedding needs to be changed, and the cow needs to be milked."

Oh. He's got his own cow, I thought. *And apparently, she must be milked every day.* Chances were, the milk I just worried about being old was inside that cow this morning. Dumbstruck by this realization, I took another gulp of the freshest glass of milk I'd ever had and decided it was delicious.

Clarence asked. "So, who should go first?"

I was eager to hear what he had to say, so I didn't hesitate. "You go first."

He let out a long sigh. "Okeydokey." He reached over to the table and picked up a pipe from the ashtray. "Mind if I have my evening smoke?"

I shook my head and squinted at the pipe he clamped between his dentures. It was a corn-cob pipe, like the one Frosty the Snowman smoked. Until that moment, I had no idea this was a real thing.

Clarence slipped a box of matches out of the bib pocket of his overalls, slid it open, plucked one out, and struck it. He held it over the bowl and took a few puffs, then sat back and blew out a cloud of smoke. "Let's see. I reckon I need to start at the beginning."

I ate another blackberry and leaned back in the armchair. The tobacco's pleasant scent reminded me of Grandpa when I was young, before he quit smoking.

Out of the blue, I felt a stab of guilt. This is me, getting cozy, eating snacks, while my brothers were going through God knows what. I told myself not to think that way. No way had I forgotten them.

Clarence wiped his fingers slowly across his brow, as if he was working up the nerve to speak. "My parents were the first white settlers in this valley. Not long before that, Ohio was Indian country. In these parts, it was Delaware Indians...until the white people pushed them out.

"After my parents came, everyone who followed was Amish. By the time I was born, this entire valley was an Amish settlement, plus us, smack dab in the middle. We got along just fine. All my friends were Amish. Our family helped them with their farming, and they helped us in return."

Clarence crossed his legs at the ankle, drawing my eye to the hole in each sock at the ball of his foot.

"The Amish tend to keep to themselves, though, so there were limits to how close we got. But like the rest of us, some Amish people gossip, which meant we kept a pretty good pulse on what was going on around here.

"I knew Eli Yoder when I was young, but I didn't pal around with him because he was ten years older than me. When he got married...well, that's when the trouble started." Clarence paused and frowned. "Martha came from a neighboring church district."

I cocked an eyebrow. "Martha?"

He nodded. "That was her given name. But within days of the wedding, she started insisting everyone call her Bertha."

There was an extended pause as Clarence puffed on his pipe. Letting him proceed on his own time, I busied myself by tilting my blackberry bowl and watching the remaining berries roll around.

"This caused a big ruckus. They only used biblical names in the local congregation, and Bertha ain't a biblical name. So, nobody wanted to call her that unless the church leadership approved. They wouldn't go along with it, though.

"It's funny to think about it now. I mean, them thinking it was a big deal how she wanted to be called by a name that ain't biblical. It's so fiddling compared to what would come later."

He uncrossed his legs, then drummed his fingertips on his knee for a spell before continuing. "Stuff started happening in the valley. I was only eleven or twelve at the time, and I wasn't Amish, so I probably didn't know the half of it in the first place. If I did, I forgot the details.

"But one thing I do remember from those days is when livestock started going missing. Pigs, sheep, cows, goats. One family would have something disappear and never show up. A little while later, the next family would lose an animal, then another. This went on for some time.

"One day, a couple of church ministers came here to see if this had happened to us. Pop told them no. They also asked families in the neighboring church districts, but they said no, too.

"The ministers decided members of the congregation were being singled out, and they somehow connected it to the name change hoopla. They decided maybe it *wasn't* such a big deal if Martha went by Bertha, after all."

Clarence let out a humorless chuckle. "Well, wouldn't you know it, after people started calling her Bertha, the livestock stopped disappearing."

He gazed across the room, focused on nothing, like he was playing things back in his head. "My sisters weren't so lucky, though."

My heart leaped into my throat. I pressed my fingers against my lips and waited for him to go on.

"I was thirteen when it happened. Alice and Catherine were eleven."

He blinked and turned his eyes to me. "They were twins."

A knot twisted in my gut.

"Identical," he added with a grim face, before I could get the question out.

The knot in my gut clenched tighter.

"It was October. Harvest time. The busiest time on the farm. Everyone in the family worked from sunup to sundown, when we'd all be beat. We'd sleep like the dead.

"In the middle of the night, something woke me up with a jolt. I shot into a sitting position, trying to sort out what had happened. Then I heard a scratching sound on the tin roof above my ceiling, and it hit me. Something had thumped on the roof. My heart went into a gallop.

"I looked over at Floyd, my older brother. He lay still in his bed. I whispered his name, but Floyd was down for the count. What I really wanted to do was yell for my parents, but I was too old for that. Too chicken to get out of bed, too. So, I just sat there." Clarence's face seemed to sag as he thought back on the memory.

"The scratching sound faded away until all I could hear was my heart thumping. As the minutes passed, and I heard nothing else, my heartbeat settled. I told myself I had imagined it all, and it was time to lie back down. I did, but I was wide awake.

"At some point, I heard the hens clucking in their coop out back, the way they do when they hear someone coming. I forced myself to get up, tiptoed to the window, and pressed my face against the glass, forming a light shield with my hands around my eyes. I thought I saw something shadowy slip into the cornrows."

Clarence stopped speaking. He stared at the floor, holding the pipe with one hand, anxiously wiping his other palm over the thigh of his overalls.

"The hens settled down. My breath steamed the windowpane as I watched for five minutes or more. Nothing else moved in the night, so I decided it had been a trick of the moonlight. I went to my bed, tucked myself under the covers, and tried to relax. Gradually, I fell back asleep.

"A commotion across the hall woke me up at daybreak. It was Ma, wailing from across the hall." Clarence's voice frayed. He tapered off, and the parlor fell silent, except for the mantle clock, ticking in a steady beat.

An ache spread through my chest. I already had a sense of where this was going. Part of me needed him to continue, but part of me dreaded hearing it, because I knew there'd be no happy ending.

"Pop burst into our room, calling our names with a panicky voice. He yelled, 'Your sisters! Have you seen them?' Floyd and I sat up with our mouths hanging open, trying to shake the sleep out of our heads.

"When we both said no at the same moment, Pop turned and sprinted down the hall. The floor shook as he leaped down the stairway, three steps at a time. The screen door slammed after Pop flew out of the house.

"Floyd threw off his covers and rushed into the hallway. I followed him. It was cold when we entered my sisters' room. Mama was on her knees, sobbing, under the window ledge. The window was wide open. That made no sense because it was chilly outside. Their bedcovers lay piled on the floor.

"My sisters were missing, and their window was wide open. I suddenly understood why my parents were so upset."

Goosebumps spread down my arms as my mind flashed back to Bertha, leading my brothers out of their tent. I blinked repeatedly, trying to suppress the tears I felt welling up in my eyes, but I resisted the urge to interrupt Clarence about what had happened to me. It was his turn to tell his story. My turn would come.

Clarence cleared his throat, then continued in a somber voice. "My family never forgot the way our Amish neighbors supported us. They dropped their harvesting duties. The men organized search parties, while the women prepared food, setting up a long row of tables in our barn for meals. They were so much more helpful than the sheriff.

"That day passed like a blur. Before we knew it, the sun was setting. Without a trace of Alice or Catherine." Clarence spoke the last phrase haltingly, looking sickly, as if merely saying it tore open the old scar.

I wanted to say something comforting, but I was speechless. All I could do was grit my teeth and fiddle with the end of the robe's belt while waiting for him to continue.

"Each day that followed, our hope dwindled. Mama became despondent. Pop looked like he was lugging the world on his shoulders. Before long, Thanksgiving Day arrived. There were no grateful feelings in this house—only grief. A huge gaping hole had been ripped in our family. Christmas Day and New Year's Day were as grim as all the other days. It was the winter that never ended."

Clarence pulled a handkerchief out of his bib pocket, lifted his glasses, and dabbed his eyes. After tucking it away, he took a puff from his pipe and slowly blew it out.

"On a cold day in late February, Pop found Mama hanging in the barn."

I covered my mouth with my palm. This latest bombshell left me feeling as though I'd been kicked in the head. Sitting inside that poor woman's house, I could feel her pain, so close by, so raw.

Clarence dropped his gaze to the floor, suddenly looking like a very old man. "She was only 36 years old." His voice cracked. "Whatever was left of Pa's heart was broken that day, and it gave out completely three years later. He died in his sleep. I was the one who found him."

Closing his eyes, Clarence fell into an extended silence. Eventually, he sniffed, then went on, speaking in a hushed voice. "Floyd and I lived together, alone, for a couple years. But when I turned eighteen, Floyd moved to Youngstown and took a job in the coal mines. I reckon he couldn't take it here anymore. Can't blame him."

With a heavy breath, Clarence tapped the pipe out in the ashtray, laid it on its side, then leaned back onto the couch.

"A year after Floyd left, the next set of twins disappeared. This time, it was a pair of Amish boys in another church district, a few miles away. Twins, of course. Identical. Twelve years old. It was much the same story as Alice and Catherine's. They vanished in the night while the family was sleeping.

"I joined the search parties. I could sense the community's fear. The men were saying it was the work of Satan.

"I don't know when the Amish began outwardly distrusting Eli and Bertha Yoder, but I definitely picked up on it during the search parties. The Yoders were keeping their distance. They hadn't gotten involved when my sisters went missing, either.

"Needless to say, those twin boys were never seen again. As you'd expect, the terror level in the valley rose another notch."

As I hung on Clarence's words, I rubbed the doily's lacework with the tip of my pinky, the only finger not stained with blackberry juice.

The feel of it gave me comfort. Maybe it helped keep me grounded in the present.

"A few months later, a two-headed calf was born on one of the neighboring farms, and all hell broke loose. The Amish tend to be superstitious. The congregation took that two-headed calf as a sign from God. Not a *good* sign, either.

"Me? I didn't think it was a sign of anything. These things happen now and again. A freak of nature, that's all. But there was plenty of other stuff going wrong around here. Nothing but bad business in this valley.

"After that two-headed calf arrived, the first family left. Abandoned their house and fled. It's a big deal for an Amish family to leave their congregation because they can't simply join another church. They're put in some form of exile. But the local bishop bent over backward to help that family join another church. I reckon he didn't blame them for running away."

Clarence's shoulders slumped, and he went perfectly still. It seemed like time froze, except the clock continued to tick. A minute or more passed before he continued.

"Around that time, I met Bessie in the closest town, Moravian Village, and we were married a few months later. Newlywed me was over the moon. But as happy as I was, and as nice as it was not living alone in this house anymore, it seemed like there was a black cloud hanging over the valley.

"Over the next couple years, we heard rumors about tension among the Amish. Eli and Bertha had no kids, and we always suspected maybe the Amish thought there was something wrong with that. But no kids came for us either, so the way we saw things, sometimes it ain't meant to be. No, the problem was much worse than that.

"You see, the Amish hold church every other Sunday, but they've got no dedicated place of worship. Instead, service is hosted by each family in the church district on a rotating basis. Usually, it's held in a barn. Hosting church is a lot of work, so the elders are relieved of the duty.

"The church service lasts about three hours, followed by a meal, which lasts for a few more hours. If a family is being disciplined by church leadership, they ain't allowed to stay for the meal. If things are really bad, they're forced to sit in a different room during church services. They call these treatments being 'in the bann,' and in their close-knit communities, they can be real good forms of discipline.

"Often, these punishments are dished out to families who don't follow the church's restrictions on modern conveniences. By the way, the English—that's what the Amish call non-Amish—often think the Amish view such things as evil, but that ain't quite right. They view them as distractions from a simple life, and they believe a simple life helps them stay spiritual.

"The bishop of each congregation sets the rules about which modern conveniences are allowed, so they vary a lot from one church district to the next. The rules don't necessarily make sense to us English. But the point is, the rules are the rules, and they're supposed to be followed and not questioned.

"Somewhere along the line, when it was Eli and Bertha Yoder's turn to host church, they refused. The ministers put them in the bann. But it had no effect. For a few years, this became the norm: the Yoders never hosted church, never stayed to eat, and always sat in a separate room during service.

"People started talking about something fishy: Eli was looking older. Wrinkle lines were showing on his face. Streaks of gray appeared in his beard. But Bertha? She looked no older than the day they married. The only thing that had changed was her eyes."

My scalp prickled as my hair stood on end. "Oh, my God," I said, balling my hands into fists and pressing them against my mouth. "I know about that."

Clarence gave me a weary look. "Cloudy and yellow?"

I nodded. "Sorry," I said. "Please go on."

He raised a finger. "Hold on a second." He dug into his bib pocket and pulled out the box of matches. Grunting as he pushed up from the couch, he crossed the room, struck a match, and lit the oil lamp beside me. Although I had hardly noticed it was getting dark, the glow it cast made me feel a little better.

After lighting the other lamp on the end table beside his seat, Clarence settled back onto the couch. "Well, at some point, a third set of identical twins went missing."

I swallowed what felt like a hot coal in my throat. Somehow, I felt blindsided hearing this. Why was Ungodly taking all these twins? I hated her more than ever.

"This time, it was ten-year-old girls from yet another church district—one even further away, in the opposite direction. But the local congregation could clearly see they were at the center of the pattern. Two more families picked up and left the valley.

"The Yoders stopped attending church altogether. People started talking openly about how the devil got into Bertha. Word spread to the neighboring congregations about the wayward member of this settlement.

"A group of Amish bishops from the wider region started meeting, trying to decide what to do about the 'Yoder problem.' Eventually, the decision was made to excommunicate the Yoders. Five bishops were given the task of telling Eli.

"These five bishops went to his farm. Before they could knock on the door, Eli met them on the porch. When they gave him the news, they heard Bertha cackle from inside the house. Eli just shrugged and told them to leave."

Clarence paused to pick out a few unpopped popcorn kernels, which he dropped into his ashtray. Beside me, the oil lamp gave off a soft crackling sound, adding to my tension.

"Things calmed down for a few years. Until the next set of twins disappeared, that is. These were twelve-year-old English boys from Moravian Village. Bessie knew the family, so it hit her hard. Even though they weren't Amish, and they lived some distance away, a sense of dread snowballed through this valley. The locals were saying evil was in their midst. Three more families picked up and moved.

"All of Homer County was on edge. Yeah, most of the kids who had gone missing were Amish, but when those twin English boys vanished, people knew this weren't just an Amish problem.

"There was a lot of pressure on the sheriff to solve these crimes, and wouldn't you know it, a lifelong village scoundrel was soon arrested, charged, and indicted?

"In the court of public opinion, the sheriff had caught his guy. Even I felt better, as desperate as I was for justice to be served. The local Amish were relieved, too. But as it turned out, they had nothing on that rascal. 'Not guilty,' the jury said. We all should've known it was poppycock."

Clarence pushed his glasses up onto his forehead and rubbed the bridge of his nose for a while, like he was working up the nerve to continue. With an audible breath, he lowered his glasses back into place and went on.

"A couple more local families picked up and left the valley. By this point, at least one out of every four Amish households had moved away. That's when the people still living here started saying the valley was cursed. They started calling it 'Forgotten Valley.'

"The bishops put their heads back together and decided it wasn't enough to excommunicate the Yoders. The only way the community would find peace was if they left the region. Money was pooled together from the surrounding congregations, and those same five bishops made another visit to the farm, prepared to offer a pretty penny for the property.

"Hah. Fat chance of that. Once again, Eli met them on the front porch, this time with a shotgun. Once again, Bertha cackled from the house when one man called out their offer. This time, Eli leveled his gun at them when he told them to leave. A few weeks later, poof. One of those five bishops went missing. People knew the Yoders had something to do with it. But they had no way of proving it."

Clarence let out a long sigh, then continued. "There was another local family with young twins, born shortly after my sisters were taken. Boys. They lived a few farms down yonder. I didn't want to tell that family what to do, but I had a bad feeling, so I asked the father if he was thinking about leaving. He told me he was putting his faith in God, and he asked me to pray. I wanted to shake him.

"Well, you know what they say? God helps those who help themselves. Those poor boys were sitting ducks, and when they were twelve, they disappeared in the dead of night. It was 1915 when this happened."

Clarence snapped his fingers. "This was the straw that broke the camel's back. Over the next few years, every remaining Amish house in this valley was abandoned. The nickname Forgotten Valley became true. Ever since then, it was just us. Now, it's just me. And *them.*"

The oil lamp beside me crackled, but Clarence said no more. No longer feeling like I had to brace myself, a tiny bit of my tension drained away.

Eventually, I asked Clarence, "Why didn't *you* leave?"

He swept his hand across the room. "This was our home. The only home I ever knew. My brother was my only family left. But working in the coal mines, bad luck followed him. He got black lung disease and barely outlived Pa." He gave a weak shrug. "So, where would I go?"

Even though he asked it like a question, it wasn't, so I didn't bother to respond.

"And anyway, I never really felt Bessie and me were at risk. It was the kids they were after."

Twins, I thought, *Identical twins, to be exact,* with a sick feeling in my gut.

Chapter 20

CLARENCE FOLDED HIS ARMS and leaned back on the couch. "Alrighty, Missy. That's my story. It's your turn to spill the beans."

I responded with a forced smile and tried to sound lighthearted. "It's like we're trading scary campfire tales."

He bobbed his head from side to side and faked a smile of his own. "It ain't as fun when they're true."

With a sigh, I shifted in my seat.

I started by describing the backpacking trip with Dad, and how he was withering away with ALS now. I explained that I was taking my brothers on the same outing and told him about what had happened at the campsite: the bullfrogs, the figure dressed in black, and how she had led my brothers out of their tent and into the pond.

When I mentioned the wolves, Clarence held up his hand to cut me off. "Are you sure they were wolves?"

"Definitely. When I saw them, I immediately thought, 'Seriously? There are no wolves in Ohio.'"

Clarence shook his head. "They were all killed off even before I was born. But here's the thing: before all the Amish people left the valley, sometimes people would claim to see wolves. I never seen one myself. I always reckoned they'd seen wild dogs or coyotes."

"Hold that thought," I said with a raised finger. "We'll come back to the wolves."

I talked through how Bertha and my brothers climbed back out of the pond, and how I chased them through the woods and down the country road, taking the time to include the detail about how the word "Ungodly" had been scratched onto that sign under the Yoders' mailbox.

Clarence gave a genuine chuckle when he heard that. "Ungodly is right," he said. "I reckon some of the Amish boys did that before moving out."

"I nicknamed her Ungodly in my thoughts," I told him.

"It surely fits."

"The name Bertha does, too."

Clarence laughed again. "I'll say. And to think she chose that name herself."

I explained how my brothers had been dressed like Amish boys and how they magically started speaking Pennsylvania Dutch. Then, I played back the scene in the woods. Eli. The twin girls. The fire. The singing.

When I described how Ungodly cut out the twin women's tongues, Clarence gasped and covered his mouth. I felt so bad because it wasn't a big leap to conclude his sisters had met the same fate. I paused to let him collect himself.

I eventually went on, telling him how Ungodly had turned the twin women into wolves.

Clarence scratched his head. "So that's where the wolves come from?"

"I think so. But I have a theory. We'll come back to it."

I explained how Eli knocked me out and chained me in the henhouse, and I described seeing Bertha perched on the roof in the thunderstorm. Clarence's jaw hung open while I told him about how she'd been struck by lightning, yet not only survived, but was somehow energized by it.

I talked through how I discovered the bones under the chicken coop and played back how I escaped, what I'd done to Eli, and how he shot me before I ran off. I wrapped up by concluding it was nothing but fear for my brothers and the last of my adrenaline that propelled me across the hayfield.

"At first, I wasn't sure you'd make it," Clarence said. "You looked like something the cat dragged in."

"You did well, Doctor Clarence." I looked over my shot-up calf. Having switched from morphine to the much less potent aspirin, my entire leg throbbed. But the swelling had gone down, and the pockmarks had closed themselves up during the eight hours since he had pulled out the shot.

"I lost track," I said. "How many sets of twins went missing?"

He silently counted them up. "I knew of five. Starting with my sisters and ending with those sitting duck boys from the local church district in 1915."

"So, the last one you knew of was forty years ago," I said.

Clarence closed his eyes for a stretch, then let out a sigh when he opened them. "I let myself believe the curse had ended. But the moment you told me your brothers were twins, I knew that was hogwash."

I nodded. "She just found another way to get her victims."

"You can't get caught if you're taking kids from a different era."

"It's the perfect crime," I said, feeling dumbstruck by it all.

Clarence put his hands on his knees and leaned forward. "You know, when you told me you came from 2025, I thought the painkillers had turned your head to mush."

"Really? You never questioned me."

"Well, I didn't think I could've swayed you."

"But now you believe me?"

"Undoubtedly. Once we put it together, it all makes sense." He finished off his last blackberry and placed the bowl on the end table. "Well, I don't mean to say any of it makes sense..."

"I know what you mean."

Clarence fixed his eyes on the wall behind me and chewed the inside of his cheek. "I always suspected Eli was behind the kidnappings. But based on what you saw, it ain't Eli taking those kids."

I sucked in a long breath and blew it out slowly. "It was Bertha all along."

"Seems so. The question is, how does she get them to go willingly?"

"She puts them under some sort of spell," I said. "Like a witch."

Clarence wrung his hands, looking stricken at the word.

"Wait..." I leaned forward and asked, "There's something else: Do you know witches age more slowly?"

He shook his head. "I know diddlysquat about witches. I always thought of that as fairy tale stuff."

I pursed my lips. "I would have said so too before the last few days."

"Good point. So, how do you know about witches?"

"I learned some folklore when I wrote a report on the Salem witch trials for history class. I love that sort of thing." Then I corrected myself: "Loved. Past tense."

"So, witches don't grow old?"

"They do, but very slowly."

I put the last blackberry in my mouth and let it dissolve on my tongue as I thought through all that had happened and everything

Clarence had told me. One particular question gnawed at me. Eventually, I came out and asked it. "Why does she need identical twins?"

Clarence froze for a moment, then pointed at the bookshelf behind me. "My parents had a book about twins. It's probably still on one of those shelves. Anyway, they used to read it to us. Alice and Catherine couldn't get enough of that book." He stared off for a moment with a wistful smile, which soon faltered before fading away. "Identical twins have a long history in mythology. It's believed they have special powers. Some of these powers involve health and healing."

"Well, there you go," I said.

Clarence arched his brows and studied me, anticipating the punchline.

I went on. "She goes after these health and healing powers. That's how she keeps herself young."

He rubbed his chin. "So, twins are like her fountain of youth."

"And that would explain why she takes another pair every six or seven years," I added.

I thought through the ritual I had witnessed. My skin crawled at the memory of how she had eaten those girls' tongues. But then, it clicked. I wagged my pointer finger in the air. "She takes their life *through their tongues.*"

We locked eyes, and I saw Clarence's Adam's apple bob as he swallowed.

My blood went cold thinking about that awful, outstretched tongue, but then, another piece fell into place. "And that's why hers is so long. It grows with each pair of twins."

Then, something Eli had said came back to me. "There's another thing. I had almost forgotten it..."

Clarence gave me a wary look, like questioning whether he wanted to hear any more.

"Eli had referred to her as 'they.' And 'them.' He told me, 'they' took my brothers. He said, 'they' will decide what to do with them. I didn't understand it at the time. I never saw anyone else, and I didn't think it was a gender-neutral pronoun thing."

"A what?"

I waved it off, wishing I hadn't mentioned it. "Never mind. He called her 'them' because when Bertha eats their tongues, she absorbs them. I mean, she absorbs their energy...their youth...their health...their *life.*"

Clarence dropped his gaze and stared blankly at the floor. "So, a little part of them lives on in her?"

Recalling how Ungodly's scream sounded like a chorus of shrieks, I raised my hands, palms up. "It makes sense, doesn't it?"

He chewed on his lower lip as he considered this, then began nodding slowly.

"And if so," I added, "they're probably locked under her spell forever."

After a long, silent moment, Clarence said, "Then their souls won't find rest until she's dead."

With that idea hanging in the air, for the first time, I realized it wasn't enough to save my brothers. Not for all the twins that came before them.

Eventually, Clarence resumed talking through the process. "At some point, she gets hold of a new pair of twins, and the whole thing repeats."

I thought about how Xavier and Dustin were doing chores such as weeding and hanging laundry. "Maybe she keeps the new pair around for a while, in a trance." Could this mean my brothers might not be in immediate danger? As comforting as I found that idea, I couldn't count on it. We had nowhere near enough information to establish a pattern. "Is it possible that for some, at least, she waits until they're adults?"

Clarence rubbed the back of his neck as he mulled this over. "You know, the local Amish got baptized when they turn eighteen."

When he said that word, I slapped my thigh, suddenly remembering how Bertha had poured water over the girls' heads. "That's what it was!"

Clarence narrowed his eyes. "What was?"

"At the fire, before she cut off their tongues, she poured water over their heads. It was a baptism!"

Clarence's head lolled, as if the idea disoriented him. He steadied himself and blew out a puff of breath through his lips. "That's one *corrupt* baptism. I mean, a baptism is a vow. But she had them under a spell. That ain't free will."

Neither of us spoke for a while, as if we had to come to grips with this. The gentle hiss of the oil lamps and the steady ticking of the mantle clock were the only sounds in the room until Clarence broke the silence. "So, is Eli just a bystander in all this?"

I ran my hands through my hair as I thought it over. "He wasn't the one taking the kids. But he still goes along with it."

Then I remembered something from my high school research on the Salem witch trials. I sat upright and looked Clarence in the eye. "He's her *familiar.*"

He squinted. "Her what?"

"Her familiar. Witches have helpers. Companions. They're called familiars. They protect the witch. Eli is Bertha's familiar."

"These familiars...they're people?"

"They can be. Long ago, people thought they were demons, sent by the devil to assist the witch. They took the form of animals. But in more modern times, folklore says that ordinary humans can be familiars, too."

"Geez. You sure know a lot about this stuff."

I held up my hand to show a small gap between my forefinger and thumb. "Just a little. By the way, vampires have familiars, too."

Clarence frowned. "Vampires?"

"Sorry, we don't need to worry about vampires."

He let out a nervous laugh. "I sure hope not. We've got our hands full with a real-life witch."

Clarence picked a few pieces of popcorn out of his bowl and tossed them into his mouth. I followed his lead, even though at that moment, it didn't seem right to be eating popcorn. That's what you do when you're watching a movie, but *nothing* about this topic was entertaining.

Tasting the bacon grease flavor, I understood why Clarence thought this was the best way to pop it. But if Mom had a taste, she would complain about what it was doing to her cholesterol.

"So, if Eli is Bertha's familiar," Clarence said, pulling me back into the moment, "he's doing these things because he's loyal to her."

I thought back to my interactions with Eli. "Right. But at times it seemed like he felt bad for me."

Clarence steepled his hands and pressed them against his mouth. "Could be he doesn't have a choice."

I shrugged about this idea of a reluctant familiar. "Maybe he's under her control, too. Like the twins."

We fell back into an uneasy silence until Clarence cleared his throat, twisted up his face, and asked, "So, what became of my sisters?"

"That brings me back to my theory," I said, and I began talking it through. "When Bertha cut out their tongues..."

Clarence bristled.

"I'm sorry."

"No," he said, giving me an apologetic wave. "Go on."

"When Bertha cut out their tongues, she took their lives. She used witchcraft to transform what was left of them into wolves. But those wolves weren't actual wolves. They were more like zombies."

Clarence cocked his head. "Zombies?"

"I mean, they're soulless. They were her physical creations, molded from the twins' remains. And the way they were trying to keep me from her, those wolves were her familiars, too."

Clarence furrowed his brow as he considered this. "So, if the twins were turned into wolves, that ain't their bones under the henhouse."

"Bingo. If I had to guess, there were half a dozen skeletons down there. They were probably people the Yoders had viewed as threats over the years.

Clarence rubbed his chin. "Like that bishop who went missing."

"Most likely," I said.

"So that's what became of him. Poor fella."

"And chances are, if I hadn't escaped..." I trailed off.

But Clarence finished my thought. "You would've joined them, too."

Chapter 21

I woke up to the smell of fried eggs and bacon, which immediately made my stomach growl.

Noticing how bright the sun was streaming through the window, I knew I had slept in late. But I was stunned to discover that the wind-up clock on my nightstand read 10:15—way later than I would have ever expected.

As I pushed myself upright on the edge of the bed in what had been Bessie's bedroom, I was glad to find my injuries were less sore than the night before. Although Clarence had assured me that I'd recover quickly, I was still preparing for much worse.

I gave my leg and shoulder an inspection and was pleased to see that the swelling was mostly gone, a healthy pink tone had returned to my skin, and the dimples were scabbing over.

When I looked in the bathroom mirror, I had that puffy morning face you get after an extra-long night of sleep. I rinsed my face with several handfuls of cold water, hoping it would help.

Next, I brushed my teeth. I had gotten past the initial shock of using Bessie's mangy old toothbrush with baking soda as toothpaste, and it helped to remind myself how I would have killed for such a luxury during my time in the henhouse.

"Good morning," I said, walking into the kitchen wearing Bessie's plaid cotton housedress with a collar and big buttons down the front. I felt like a kid playing dress-up.

Clarence, glancing up from the frying pan, flashed me his pearly dentures in a broad smile. He made a point of looking away quickly, which honestly helped make me more comfortable. I told myself that, as tough as it was for me to be wearing this outfit, it would be tougher on him seeing me in his late wife's clothes.

With the spatula, he gestured to the open table. "Pour yourself a cup of coffee."

I almost passed on the coffee, having weaned myself off it in the weeks leading up to the hike, since I'd have to do without while camping. Dad had done this on our trip, so I learned the trick from him. With a shrug, I poured a cup from the stovetop percolator and took a sip.

Being a bit of a coffee snob, I hadn't expected to like this coffee, but it tasted heavenly. Of course, maybe it was because I hadn't had coffee in almost two weeks.

Breakfast consisted of bacon, eggs, diced potatoes, and fried green tomato slices. The glass of milk that went with it was not cold, but it was rich and creamy.

"Want another cup of coffee?" Clarence offered as we finished eating.

"Yes, please, but I'll get it." I wandered over to the stove, refilled my cup, and topped his off as well.

Clarence slurped from his refilled cup. "With any luck, I'll have Trotter running this afternoon."

"Is there anything I can do to help?"

"No," he said. "It's a man's job."

That comment made my blood boil. I could have explained how I often helped Dad and Grandpa when they tuned up the GTO. I could have told him how I planned to study mechanical engineering, like Dad.

But the look on Clarence's face was pleasant and harmless. I told myself that he lived in a different time, and he meant no offense by it. Hoping I didn't need to stick around long in this era, I swallowed my indignation with a gulp of coffee and let it go.

"Once I get her running, do you still want me to take you to the hospital?"

"No," I said. It was my brothers I was worried about, not me, with my bumps and bruises all healing.

Clarence nodded. "I reckon there ain't much left for them to do. Plus, you'd be shocked at the cost of a hospital visit these days."

You have no idea, I thought, but I left it alone. Instead, I said, "We need to go to the sheriff."

Clarence raked his fingers through his sparse hair. "I've been kicking that around. What would we say?"

What would we say? I thought, incredulous. *Where do I start?*

But before I could answer, Clarence clarified his point. "First of all, the sheriff won't expect cooperation from the Amish, because that's the way it usually goes. The Amish prefer to resolve conflict within their own community, and their mindset is to let God be the judge."

I had heard things to this effect, but I still tried to make my case. "The sheriff can't ignore kidnapping cases, though."

Clarence took a swig of his coffee. "Let's play this out, then. How are you going to prove they're your brothers?"

I stared at him, trying to figure out how to respond.

He pressed his point. "They *look* Amish. They *speak* Pennsylvania Dutch. And they ain't trying to get away."

I stammered before blurting out, "Can she prove they're *her* kids?"

"She doesn't have to. Most Amish babies are delivered at home. They rarely even bother with birth certificates because in their world, they don't need them. For instance, they won't be applying for driver's licenses."

With my throat tightening, I propped an elbow on the table and leaned my forehead into my hand.

"And what's the sheriff going to think of your story, anyway? Are you going to say that you came from the year 2025?"

I clenched my eyes shut, but a few seconds later, I felt Clarence take my free hand, giving it a gentle squeeze. "I'm real sorry to say all this."

My eyes stung as they welled up with tears. I tried to blink them clear, but one got away, spilling down my cheek. I quickly wiped it dry and looked at him. "What should I do?"

"Oh, Missy," he said. "The question is, what should *we* do?"

His saying that made me want to cry even harder. I tried to talk, but the words caught in my throat.

"You ain't alone here," Clarence added, giving my hand another gentle squeeze.

I pulled away, sniffed, and sat upright. "Clarence, you've already helped me so much. You took me in. You fixed me up. You're taking care of me. You don't need to get involved in my battle."

"*Your* battle?" He crossed his arms and stared at me sharply. "I've spent over 65 years not really knowing what happened to my sisters. But what you told me last night removes all doubt. That evil thing took them, and in a roundabout way, it took my parents, too. I've got a score to settle. This ain't just your battle."

"Thank you," I said in a weak voice.

Clarence ground the knuckles of one hand into the palm of his other. "We're going to get your brothers. And mark my words, we're going to get that witch."

Chapter 22

When I finished wringing out my clothes in the cellar's galvanized laundry tub, I took one last look at the setup and shook my head in disbelief. Yeah, I had actually washed them by hand, using one of those old-timey washboards with the *MAID-RITE* brand painted above *THE COLUMBUS WASHBOARD CO., ESTABLISHED 1895.*

I pinned them to the clothesline on the back porch so they could dry in the sun, making a point of hanging my underwear on the end closest to the house, where it would be slightly less prominent. My sports bra went on full display, though, since I figured Clarence wouldn't even know what it was.

With him still in the barn piecing the carburetor back together, I went to work cleaning up the kitchen. I tried not to think about how I was doing what he'd call "a woman's job." I was making myself useful and showing some gratitude for all he had done for me.

While drying the dishes, Clarence emerged from the barn carrying the carb in one hand and a toolbox in the other. The dogs followed him toward the Studebaker. *Trotter,* I reminded myself. *Might as well call her by her name.*

Clarence worked under the hood while I put the dishes away. When I stepped out onto the back porch, I caught the screen door so it wouldn't slam, possibly the first person in Forgotten Valley to do so.

With tails wagging, all three dogs wandered across the lawn to meet me. It was hard to believe these were the same dogs that appeared so menacing when I arrived. Thank God I hadn't had that pry bar on hand.

"Hey there, Bowie," I said, giving him the first petting. "Hi, Gertie and Pepper," I added, patting both of the other dogs at the same time. I couldn't keep those two straight, but Bowie was easy, because he'd been named for the white bow tie pattern in the fur below his neck.

I gave them a gentle push, clearing some space so I could sit on the stairs. As I pulled on my boots, I turned my legs toward the barn to avoid giving Clarence a commando peep-show.

"Good news!" Clarence yelled over his shoulder. "There were no parts left over!" He let out a belly laugh.

"Nice job," I yelled back. "It doesn't always work out that way." When I was young, I took apart one of my grandfather's die-cast classic car models "for the fun of it," but when I put it back together, nothing fit tight, and I ended up with a couple of leftover pieces. I snuck it back on the shelf, and always wondered if he noticed anything amiss.

After tying my boots, I stood up to examine my getups and almost laughed out loud. I looked like a real hillbilly, wearing hiking boots with a housedress.

Clarence was tightening the nuts on the carb's mounting studs when I approached.

The dogs wandered off for a nap, and I stood back observing as Clarence went about reconnecting everything. He fussed with the throttle cable linkage for a while before letting out a huff in frustration. Stepping back, he wiped the sweat off his forehead with a greasy rag, then stared at the carb while scratching his head.

Without thinking, I leaned under the hood, flipped the linkage around, and snapped it into place.

Clarence turned to me with wide eyes and his jaw hanging open. "Well, I'll be a son of a gun!" He gave me a wide grin. "How'd you know how to do that?"

I smiled back. "Just a lucky guess."

"Well, see if you can tighten that inside stud nut better than I could."

I picked up the 9/16-inch box wrench and managed to turn it a quarter turn further than he had, since my smaller wrist fit more easily around the fuel line.

Clarence let out a chuckle. "Think you can get that choke cable connected?"

I took it like he was testing me. "This thing's got a manual choke?"

Clarence looked at me funny. "Sure does. This ain't no Cadillac!"

I found an unconnected flexible cable with a hooked wire hanging onto nothing. When I located the choke arm, I threaded the hook into the hole.

"Well done, Missy!" He patted me on the back, then began gathering his tools, placing them into his toolbox. "Care to put the air cleaner back on?" He gestured behind me with his chin, and when I turned around, I discovered the filter housing on the ground behind the front wheel. I lifted it over the carb and lined up the bolt to the hole in the cover, then spun the wing nut into place.

"Much obliged. Saved me a bit of back strain," Clarence said, nodding his approval. "You're an old pro at this."

"Think she'll start?" I asked.

He gave a nervous laugh. "Could go either way. Do you want the honor?"

Without answering, I walked around to the driver's side and pulled open the door. Before climbing in, I looked over the sparse interior. The steel dashboard, painted the same blue as the exterior but coated in road dust, had just a few gauges and knobs, clustered behind the enormous steering wheel. The keys dangled from the ignition.

I slid behind the bus-sized steering wheel, desperately hoping the engine would start. My palms were sweating, so I wiped them dry on my dress.

It took me a minute to orient myself on the barren-looking dash. When I saw three pedals on the floor, I knew it had a manual transmission, but there was no gear shifter on the floor hump. I found a chrome handle behind the steering wheel and remembered my dad telling me about the old "three on the tree" transmissions. After confirming the parking brake was engaged, I wiggled the shifter into neutral.

With a serious look on his face, Clarence held up both hands with his fingers crossed. I flashed my own crossed fingers at him, pushed in the aluminum knob on the dashboard to close the choke, pressed the gas pedal once to prime it, and turned the ignition.

My heart pounded as the starter cranked. It chugged away for a while without firing. Knowing the bowl was empty from the carb rebuild, I pumped the gas pedal and kept on cranking. I started feeling sick with the realization that the motor might not fire.

But out of the blue, it sputtered once, twice, then a third time. With that spark of hope, I kept on cranking until suddenly, the engine roared to life.

Clarence and I exchanged euphoric thumbs-ups. "She's purring like a kitten!" he yelled over the rumble.

Before long, the engine started to starve from a lack of oxygen, so I pulled the choke knob halfway out. The motor settled into a smooth idle, and when it began faltering again a short while later, I fully opened the choke. The engine settled into a steady rhythm and stayed there.

"Should we go for a reconnaissance mission ride now, or after supper?" Clarence asked through the open window.

"Let's go now," I said, anxious to get a lay of the land, so we could start working out our rescue operation. "We'll work out our plans after dinner."

When he gave me a questioning look, I corrected myself. "After *supper.*" Apparently, in Homer County, the word "dinner" wasn't the same as "supper." Whatever.

Clarence slammed the hood closed, and when he returned to where he had been standing, he asked, "Wanna drive?"

I hesitated. Driving this truck with a three-speed transmission would be a challenge I didn't feel like I needed.

On the other hand, Clarence was eighty years old. My great-grandmother had gotten into two car accidents around that age, before she finally agreed to give up driving altogether. But when I considered there'd be zero traffic, that clinched it. "You can drive," I said, sliding across the dusty bench seat to the passenger side. "You know the neighborhood."

Clarence climbed in, and we were soon rolling down the sloping driveway, gravel popping under the tires.

All three dogs appeared out of nowhere, bounding after the truck. Clarence skidded to a stop and got out to open the tailgate. After they hopped into the truck bed, we continued on.

When Clarence turned onto the single-lane gravel roadway, I looked around to get my bearings. "Isn't Bertha's lair the other way?" I asked, pointing over my shoulder through the rear window.

"It is," Clarence said. "I want to get a little test drive in. Make sure she's running well."

Fair enough, I thought. *We don't need to be stalling out in Ungodly's parts.*

We passed beyond the edge of Clarence's farm and entered a stretch of forest.

Clarence chuckled. "*Bertha's lair.* I had to think about that one. It fits."

"Yeah," I said without humor. "It doesn't seem right calling it a home."

Clarence punched the gas a few times, revving the engine, but mostly spinning the rear tires on the gravel. After the third time, he patted the top of the dashboard. "She's running like a dream. Steadier than she has in years."

I responded with a thumbs-up. It wasn't exactly a smooth ride by my standards, so I could only imagine what it was like before he rebuilt that carb. Regardless, I was happy to hear his assessment.

"This is Township Road 666," Clarence said, picking up speed.

I did a double-take. "Wait...what?"

"TR-666."

"Literally, like that's *actually* the number?"

Clarence nodded. "Yup. I hear that number has something to do with the devil. The township put numbers on the roads when I was a kid. We drew the short straw, I reckon. Mama wanted to change it, but the Township refused, so it stuck. I never believed that superstition was the root of our problems, though."

"Probably not," I said, although it sure was a weird coincidence. And it wouldn't surprise me if that number encouraged the exodus of Amish families from the valley.

Clarence spat out his open window. I cringed in disgust and turned away to look out my side.

"Anyway, TR-666 runs between two points on the state route, through Forgotten Valley. The valley is U-shaped, wrapping around a ridge. My farm is on one side of that ridge, and the Yoders are on the other. So, when you escaped and cut through the forest, you took a shortcut from way back yonder."

The wooded stretch ended, and an abandoned home and barn came into view. The peeling Amish-style house was barely visible, obscured by overgrowth. Behind it stood a rusting water pump windmill, with half of its blades missing. A gaping hole had opened up in the middle of the barn's roof. Surrounding the farm, long-fallow fields stretched out in both directions.

As we passed by the property, the ruins of another homestead appeared across the road, eerily similar to the last.

"See what I mean?" Clarence said, sweeping his hand from one to the other. "The entire valley up and left."

I nodded. "It's like a ghost town."

"Speaking of ghosts..." Clarence pointed at a split-rail fence encircling a square of overgrown grass with rows of white stones arranged within.

I asked, "Is that a cemetery?"

He nodded. "That was the local settlement's graveyard."

The headstones, all the same size and shape, were barely tall enough to peek above the untended grass. "Is Bessie buried there?"

"Nah. I'm not sure how the Amish would feel about planting an English coffin in their boneyard. Then again, maybe they wouldn't mind. But no, she's in the Moravian Village Cemetery. There's a plot waiting for me beside her."

After we passed two more farms, Clarence pointed ahead at another derelict house, tucked in behind a scrub of trees. "This here's where those sitting-duck twin boys lived." He immediately looked away, as if not seeing it might erase the memory.

I watched nervously as we passed, thinking about the heartbroken family who had lost their sons and left their home behind. Forty years later, most of the windows were broken, and one end of the front porch had collapsed.

When we came upon the next farm, I asked, "So, it's more of the same up ahead?"

He nodded. "Roundabout two more miles of it, until the road reaches the state highway."

"Let's head back the other way."

"Alrighty." He released the gas and coasted into the farm's overgrown driveway, the weeds raking Trotter's underside. The three dogs started dancing around in the truck bed, thinking they'd be getting out there.

Before shifting into reverse, Clarence gave me a sidelong look. "You sure you're up for it?"

"I'm sure," I said, turning away to examine the old house with a fallen tree propped on top of it, crumpling part of the roof.

He backed out onto the road, and in silence, we drove straight into the lingering cloud of dust we had left behind.

As we retraced our route, I rewatched the creepy progression of long-deserted farms and thought about how scared those families must have been to leave it all behind.

As if Clarence sensed my discomfort, he began whistling "Swanee River." He was a good whistler, like my great-grandfather had been.

I wondered if this was something that all the old timers did. Maybe it was becoming a lost art.

I hummed along, but quietly, since holding a tune was never one of my strong suits.

By the time we came back to his farm, the song was over. As we passed, I noticed his mailbox was dented to hell and heavily coated with rust, prompting me to ask, "Do they deliver mail to that mailbox?"

"That's a bit of a sore subject," Clarence said. "When all those Amish families moved out, the Post Office decided to stop coming through here. They made me and Bessie put up a new box on the state route." Clarence hooked his thumb over his shoulder, indicating the end where his mailbox was now located.

A minute later, he started whistling "I've Been Working on the Railroad." It seemed like he was following a standard playlist.

More deserted homes followed, but he didn't bother pointing them out. There were too many to count, but the sheer number of them drove home the valley's nickname: Forgotten Valley.

The road followed a long, sweeping bend, with a row of sandstone outcroppings lining its side at the end of the ridge. Other derelict homes appeared beyond. Clarence moved on to "On Top of Old Smokey."

When he finished that song, he didn't start another. I noticed he was slowing down the truck, and about the same time, I stiffened at the sight of the sign with the altered biblical verse hanging under the mailbox. Without even thinking about it, the words played back in my head: *KNOW THAT I AM UNGODLY.*

Without saying a word, Clarence pointed at the drive. With a lump lodged in my throat, I nodded acknowledgment. The three dogs all gathered along that side of the truck bed.

My head became a cauldron of emotions as we approached the place where my brothers were being held. Part of me wanted to curl up on the floor and hide. And yet, another part of me wanted to storm the farm right then and there, even knowing how foolish that would be without planning everything out.

Clarence coasted without braking, and as we rolled past the driveway, I peered up the slope. Late afternoon sunshine glared off the slate barn roof at the top of the hill, temporarily blinding me, but right before I lost the view up the driveway, something else caught my eye.

"Hey, did you see that?" I asked, but I already knew Clarence had been watching the road. I don't know, but maybe he didn't want to look up that driveway.

"See what?"

"I think I saw a wolf sitting in the drive, about halfway up."

"I missed it," he said. "If we drive back this way, we can look again."

"Could have been a dog," I mumbled, although I had serious doubts about that. It definitely wasn't...Sonny. I had to think about it for a moment to remember his name, even though it had been less than two days.

It dawned on me that if I had escaped down the driveway, I might've had a run-in with those sinister wolf-things.

Clarence frowned, but said nothing. He looked tense as he drove on, and he never went back to whistling.

The next part of the route looked vaguely familiar from the night I had chased after the buggy. Several times along that stretch, I checked out the back window, but if any wolves were coming after us, I couldn't see them through the plume of road dust we kicked up.

We passed another deserted farm before rounding the bend. The road straightened to reveal one more abandoned house.

I asked Clarence to slow down and scanned the stretch of sloping woods beyond. When a cleft in the hillside appeared, I pointed that way. "There it is."

Clarence coasted forward until we reached the gully, where he stopped. He looked over the area. "What is it?"

I leaned down to get a view up the rise and pointed that way. "We camped up there. She brought them down along that creek. I came this way." I pointed at the embankment I had tumbled down. "The campsite is in a clearing through that forest."

"How far?" he asked, looking up the slope.

I wrinkled my nose as I tried to play back my frantic chase through the woods. "Maybe fifteen minutes."

Clarence rubbed his chin. "Yeah, Camp Timberwood is up that way. It's a Girl Scout camp."

"That's right," I said. "Except in 2025, it's no longer a scout camp. Anyway, we pitched our tents on the back edge of that nature preserve."

Clarence faced forward and tapped his fingertips on the steering wheel. "Wanna keep going, or should we get to work on supper?"

"Is there anything else to see?"

"Yup. Plenty more abandoned farms until this end of the road meets the state highway."

"I think I've seen enough."

"I know what you mean," he said grimly. He shifted into first gear and let out the clutch. The truck lurched forward. A minute later, another deserted house appeared, and he pulled into its driveway to double back.

Watching the gully as we passed it again, I thought back on that night when everything started. It seemed like a lifetime ago. When I came crashing down that embankment, would I ever have believed the things that would follow?

After rounding the bend, we approached Bertha's driveway, and Clarence coasted to a crawl. I braced myself with both fists clenched, waiting to catch a straight view up the drive. As soon as it came, a blur of movement startled me. I yelped, reflexively ducking away from my open window even before I realized what was happening.

A wolf's head shot through the open frame, all teeth, her jaw wrenched wide. Her body slammed against the truck door with a booming thud, which I felt through the seat as much as heard.

I fell onto the middle of the bench, beyond the reach of the animal's bite. Clarence punched the gas. The engine roared, and the tires sprayed gravel, then caught a grip and lurched forward.

With her snarling head inches from me, the wolf dangled against the door, her front legs scrambling to climb in, her hind legs scratching at the door as she struggled to catch a grip.

The truck accelerated. As the seconds passed, the wolf clambered nearer, spraying me with saliva. I dropped to the floor.

Clarence swung his fist, clipping the beast's nose. She snarled at him, baring her slobbery teeth.

Then, through the rear window, I saw Bowie lunge for the wolf over the side of the truck bed. I knew when he bit her, because she let out a yowl as she jerked back through the window frame, plunging from view.

"Bowie, no!" Clarence yelled, letting off the gas. With the wolf gone, I pulled myself back onto the seat, leaning clear from the open window. I craned my neck to peer through the rear pane.

Gertie and Pepper cowered on the opposite side of the truck bed, leaving the alpha-dog to fight his own battle. Bowie perched himself on the edge of the truck bed, barking frantically.

A dark streak bolted down the ditch along the roadway, closing in fast. Although I couldn't see what it was through the cloud of road dust, I knew it had to be the second wolf. "Go!" I yelled to Clarence.

He floored it, but the truck fishtailed, and I watched in horror as the sideways force sent Bowie toppling over the side.

"Oh, my God," I screamed. "He fell out!"

Clarence let off the gas, but I heard a tortured yelp. I caught glimpses of a tussle through the dust cloud.

"Close your window," Clarence said as he rolled up his own.

I grabbed my window crank and started turning it.

Clarence brought the truck to a stop and turned around to stare through the rear window.

When I finished raising my window, I leaned against it to look out. I saw nothing through the spreading haze of road dust, but each yelp and whimper gave me the sensation of a knife stabbing me in the chest.

Feeling totally helpless, I burst into tears. I wanted to jump out, but knew there was nothing we could do to fight off the wolves. Although Bowie had saved me, I couldn't save him even if I sacrificed myself, which wasn't an option. I also knew that on his own, he didn't stand a chance against those two wolves. They were twice his size and driven by an unearthly vicious nature.

Clarence placed a hand on my shoulder, and when I turned to him, I saw the anguish in his face.

As I sobbed, Bowie's whimpers diminished, then went silent.

We sat there in stunned silence for a long stretch while the dust cloud slowly settled, bringing the trees along the roadside back into focus.

I peered out through the back window. Gertie and Pepper were both lying in the truck bed, as if they were hiding. I couldn't bring myself to look out the side at Bowie, though.

Bang! I jumped at the sudden sound of a wolf hurtling itself against my door. *Bang!*

Clarence pressed the gas, slowly this time, and the truck began rolling. I looked out the side window to see the wolves trotting beside us, licking their chops.

As we drove down the road, I stole a glance behind us. Receding in the distance, I picked out the sight of a bloodied bundle of fur in the ditch, and my heart ripped in two.

CHAPTER 23

AFTER A RESTLESS NIGHT, I woke up feeling cold.

Sunshine was streaming in the window, and it was summer. There was no air conditioning. No fan either. So, why was I chilly?

My head ached, too. I had expected to wake up feeling better than the day prior, but I definitely felt worse. It wasn't the traumatic memory of Bowie being slaughtered by Bertha's familiars, either. Physically, I felt worse.

The clock read 6:30, so it wasn't much later than sunrise. The smell of coffee wafted through the air. *Maybe that'll help me feel better,* I thought.

I crawled out from under the blankets and pushed up onto my feet, shivering as I reached for the bathrobe draped over the footboard.

As I moved, I realized my entire body ached, not just my head. My feet felt cold too, so I put on a pair of Bessie's hand-knitted socks.

What's wrong with me? I thought as I headed out for the bathroom.

I got the answer when I sat down on the toilet and discovered a rash on my thigh. A red ring encircled a red dot, smaller than my pinky nail. A bullseye rash. "Oh, shit," I whispered out loud.

Lyme disease.

Pressing both hands on my temples, I squeezed my head. I had forgotten all about the tick that had latched onto my leg, but now the memory of it came rushing back. The bullseye rash was a telltale sign of the debilitating tick-borne illness to which modern medicine often has no answer.

One of Mom's biggest fears on this backpacking trip had come true. She was terrified of the risk of Lyme disease, having read accounts of people—including many celebrities—who suffered from it.

I had rolled my eyes at Mom's worry, and now, I had it. Add it to the growing mountain of this trip's nightmares. The adventure that keeps on giving.

I shook my head in disbelief, but forced myself to continue my morning routine, starting with brushing my teeth with the baking soda.

What freaked me out more than anything about this revelation was the timing. While you would never want to find out you have Lyme disease, this couldn't have come at a worse time.

Clarence and I had worked out our rescue mission after dinner the previous night, and we were supposed to start executing this plan within hours. Now, I was sick with a fever, chills, and an aching head and body.

I shook out two aspirins from the bottle and chased them down with a swig of water from the faucet, hoping they'd help take the edge off. Then, I took a third for good measure.

"Morning," Clarence said as I appeared in the kitchen. He stood over the counter with several chunks of smoked ham and the jar of morphine in front of him. "Sleep well?"

I nodded and forced a smile, figuring there was no reason to burden him with the truth. Most likely, he would have never heard of Lyme disease anyway, and I wasn't going to give him a reason to call off our plan.

I watched Clarence carve two Xs into one of the ham chunks, then shove a morphine pill into each one.

"Are you sure two will be enough?" I asked.

"It's going to have to do," he said as he moved on to another chunk of ham. "I only have four pills left. But I reckon those creatures are half the weight of a man, so it would be like a man taking four. If it doesn't kill them, it'll at least knock them out of their senses for a while."

As he wrapped the chunks of meat in a dish towel, Clarence asked, "You're sure Eli feeds the chickens at ten o'clock?"

"That's what he told me."

"Okeydokey. Then, let's leave here at half past eight. I got Trotter mostly loaded up already, so we've got plenty of time for a good breakfast." He motioned to the stovetop percolator. "Get your morning cup while it's fresh. I'll whip up some breakfast now."

Not only was I not hungry, but I felt a tad queasy. I tried to ignore the sensation as I poured myself a cup of coffee.

All I could do was pray the aspirin would kick in soon, and it would be enough to get me through what lay ahead.

Chapter 24

My heart rate was already revving as we made our way down the country road, but when we rounded a bend and a turkey vulture appeared, scavenging in the ditch, my chest turned into a jackhammer.

Clarence let out a breath that sounded more like a punctured tire deflating, then rolled up his window. I followed his cue and raised mine.

The buzzard took flight, leaving behind what was left of Bowie. I avoided looking closely, but from what I saw, all that remained were a few scraps of fur and some picked-clean bones.

Clarence kept his eyes glued straight ahead.

Shortly after passing the area where Bowie died, I spotted Ungodly's old mailbox down the road, sending my anxiety level skyrocketing.

The aspirin had taken the edge off my fever and body aches, but with my pulse pounding in my temples, my head started feeling like it was going to split.

Clarence coasted, and as we approached the driveway, both of the wolves came sprinting down the slope, as though they'd been expecting us.

At the moment when Clarence braked to a dead stop, the closest wolf launched itself at his window, slamming against his door with a resounding thump. We both jumped, even though we saw it coming.

As she fell away, leaving a splatter of slobber on the glass, the second wolf crashed into the door, just as hard.

Moving slowly, Clarence unwrapped the dish towel, sitting on the bench seat between us. He took out one of the smaller chunks of meat, cracked his window open, and dropped it through. "Easy, girls," he said in a low voice. "Eat up your yummy snack."

From my end of the seat, I couldn't see the battle for the scrap, but I heard a vicious growl.

"Now, now, there's plenty to go around," Clarence said, dropping the second scrap out the window.

We waited with the engine idling until both wolves backed away from the truck, watching Clarence eagerly while licking their chops. He grabbed one of the bigger morphine-laced chunks, rolled down his window further, and flung it up the drive.

The wolves both pounced, but one got there first. The winner snapped at the loser with a snarl, sending her scurrying away with her tail between her legs. Clarence flicked her the second chunk, and soon, both were devouring their tainted meals.

He shrugged at me. "No need for Plan B," he said, gesturing to the shotgun he had mounted in the rear window.

"Let's hope you're right," I said.

I looked up the rutted driveway. The slate barn roof rose above the top of the slope, but there was no other sign of life.

After putting the truck in gear, Clarence gave it some gas. A short distance later, he skidded to a stop in front of the mailbox and read the sign out loud. "Know that I am ungodly." He gave me a sideways glance with a smirk. "That's about the long and short of it, I reckon."

I responded with a weak smile, appreciating his attempt to lighten the mood, but feeling too ill and too nervous to find much humor in it.

As we put some distance between us and Bertha's lair, my heart rate settled down, and my headache lessened.

Passing the gully that led to the campsite, Clarence tapped his watch. "It's ten to nine. If I drive slowly, those beasts should be down for the count by the time we loop back. We'll still have time before Eli goes to feed the hens."

I gave him a thumbs-up, and we slipped into an uneasy silence.

My chills had subsided, but now I felt a hot flash coming on instead. I wiped the sweat off my brow and went to aim a vent at my face, but there were none. Instead, this truck had vent windows, which I was familiar with from Grandpa's GTO. I unlatched it and swung it open, directing a cooling breeze toward me.

I barely noticed the other abandoned farms as we passed them. Instead, my gaze kept drifting back to the bullseye rash on my leg, now fully exposed, since I was wearing my own clothes once again.

Since Clarence hadn't said anything about it, I wondered if he hadn't noticed or was avoiding letting on that his eyes had wandered to my bare thigh. Hoping to avoid questions, I covered it with my open hand. It felt hot under my palm.

"Here's one end of TR-666," Clarence said, dragging me out of my thoughts.

When we came to a stop at the paved roadway, the dust cloud we'd stirred up from the gravel roadway caught up to us. As Clarence waited for it to clear, I noticed electric lines running along the opposite side of the state highway. "They have power here?" I asked.

"Pfft. They brought it through here a decade ago, but skipped the valley where I live. The REA was supposed to bring power to everyone, but Forgotten Valley was forgotten again."

I recalled Clarence mentioning REA when I first spoke with him, but I hadn't known what it was. "What's REA?"

"The Rural Electrification Act. The feds passed it almost twenty years ago to bring power to rural farms. Most have it by now, but not mine. Guess I can't blame them, with only two households in the whole valley. Plus, one of them's Amish. Well..."

"...not really Amish," I finished for him. "But I know what you mean."

Clarence just nodded.

As he accelerated onto the smooth asphalt surface of the two-lane highway, he patted the dashboard. "I can't believe how good she's running!"

We passed a farm with an antique pickup truck parked near the barn. A vintage red and gray tractor moved through the field, the farmer sitting in the open, without the enclosed cab I was used to seeing. It looked like a scene from a Norman Rockwell painting. I thought about my great-grandma, who was nuts about Norman Rockwell. For as long as I could remember, Mom would give her a Norman Rockwell calendar for Christmas every year, which she would hang on her refrigerator.

A few minutes later, we came upon a driveway with wooden signage stretched above announcing *CAMP TIMBERWOOD*. Clarence tossed his chin in that direction and let off the gas.

"That's it," I said. Although the setting had changed considerably, I recognized this as the point where the Buckeye Trail had crossed the road and taken us through the former Girl Scout camp.

Peering down the well-tended driveway, I saw half a dozen antique cars parked in a row on one side. Opposite sat a cute log cabin, with a sign reading, *WELCOME CAMPERS! PLEASE CHECK IN HERE!* I barely recognized the cabin as one of the sad, boarded-up structures we had hiked past on our way in. Everything had looked so different from the 1955 scene I was now viewing, this snapshot of a bygone time.

"I would've liked to have driven back there," I said, wondering what the camp looked like in its heyday.

"If it weren't summer, we might've been able to sneak in," Clarence said.

After following the winding road for a while, Clarence turned off onto a gravel turnout. "This is the opposite end of our township road." A rusty sign in the ditch spelled out *TR-666*.

He nudged the truck up to a lone mailbox with the name *C.J. HENRY* hand-painted on the side. "Might as well get my mail, since I'm here." When he opened it, the box was crammed full. He picked it out one handful at a time, piling it onto the bench seat, in place of the tainted ham.

I snuck a peek at the postmarks. They too read 1955, erasing the last shreds of doubt I had concerning Clarence and his cognitive state.

We weren't on the country road long before we came across the first abandoned farm. My leg bounced in nervous anticipation as we rolled past the peeling house, half-obscured by the trees growing into it, moss covering the roof.

Other ruins followed, and I soon lost count of them.

Eventually, we came upon the Amish cemetery that Clarence had shown me the day before, and a while later, we were passing by his farm.

My whole body tensed up as we rounded the sandstone ledge at the tip of the ridge. I knew it wouldn't be long now.

"It's after 9:20," Clarence said, tapping his watch. "Those wolves should be out cold by now."

With one hand still covering the rash, I raised the other with my fingers crossed. "Here's hoping." I barely recognized my frail-sounding voice.

Neither of us looked when we passed the site where Bowie had been killed.

Clarence began coasting when the mailbox came into view. The truck slowed down steadily until it was barely rolling when we reached the driveway. One wolf appeared, sprawled out on the side of the drive.

"Holy Moly," Clarence whispered. "It worked for her."

I gave him a jittery smile. "Hopefully the other one, too."

Clarence brought the truck to a full stop just past the driveway, then shifted into reverse. As he backed up the drive, the weeds growing between the wheel ruts began grazing the truck's underside.

The idea of parking this close to the farm had made me uncomfortable when Clarence suggested it, but he insisted the driveway was long enough that they would not hear us coming. He was probably right, but I didn't want to push our luck. I eventually relented, knowing we might need a quick getaway.

I watched through the rear window as we inched backward up the slope. "There," I whispered, pointing into the ditch on the side of the drive at the other wolf, lying on her side in the scrub.

"Good eye," Clarence said, squinting at the sight of her in his side-view mirror.

Neither wolf budged.

"Stop here," I said as we came close to the first of the pair.

Clarence killed the engine and set the parking brake. Reaching for the shotgun hanging in the rear window, he said softly, "I'll carry this for now."

I gave him the okay signal, figuring with the hasty lesson he'd given me, we were safer with it in his hands, anyway.

As we both slipped out of the truck, he whispered, "Leave the doors open."

I nodded, noting that he'd left the key in the ignition, as we had planned.

Clarence grunted as he lifted the SOHIO gas can out of the bed. I reached over to remove the long wooden box from my side.

Behind the truck, we cautiously approached the first wolf. I stood back to watch as Clarence nudged it with his foot. It shifted like a carcass.

With no evidence of it breathing, a small part of me couldn't help but feel bad for the thing, despite what these things had done to Bowie.

But as I had pointed out to Clarence, they weren't actual wolves. They were Bertha's soulless creations, formed from what was left of those twins after she took their lives. More like zombies...I don't know...just not wolves.

A short walk further up the drive, Clarence paused to nudge the second not-a-wolf. It too appeared to be dead. Saying nothing, he circled it and continued up the driveway.

My mind turned back to what had happened to Bowie, and I glowered at the thing, suddenly wishing we could blast it with the shotgun. But we had to avoid alerting Eli, which would screw up everything. I pulled away and hurried to catch up with Clarence.

As we neared the top of the drive, he signaled for me to take the lead. Although I felt weak and winded, and I hated the idea of returning to this place, I kept my mind on my brothers and pushed myself onward.

But when I got my first glimpse of the barn and henhouse, the full brunt of the trauma I had endured here came rushing back.

Chapter 25

It took everything in me not to turn and run from this place of horror. I told myself to calm down, set my jaw, and crept closer.

Halting where the strip of trees ended, I leaned on my knees and peeked out from the cover at Bertha's lair. My eyeballs throbbed with my pounding pulse, so I had to wait for my vision to clear.

A furry lump on the porch brought me a welcome rush of relief: Sonny had survived the shotgun blast, too. I saw no other signs of life.

Finding myself in the same place as I'd been a few nights prior, I thought about how this occasion seemed riskier in broad daylight. Clarence and I had debated it, and ultimately, agreed it was best to come here in daylight. Who knew if Bertha even slept?

And then there's that witching hour thing, the time when witches are most active. I was pretty sure this occurred in the middle of the night. Once I got to thinking about it, maybe it had been the witching hour when Bertha appeared on the roof.

We also discussed how witches might have a night-vision advantage, similar to that of cats. I told Clarence about how our mean cat, Dinah, had a way of terrorizing me when I'd walk through the darkened house. Even though I couldn't see her, she'd see me, and when I'd least expect it, she'd hiss and swipe at my feet with her claws.

Seeing no movement, I crouched and scuttled across the short clearing. Before I made it to the henhouse, Sonny lifted his head and looked our way.

I ducked behind the chicken coop, and Clarence arrived seconds later. He leaned against the siding as he tucked the gas can into the long grass beside the structure. The hens clucked softly in response, and a moment later, Sonny came around the corner, wagging his tail.

Clarence made a cringy face.

I shrugged, scratched Sonny's head, and whispered. "Sorry, buddy, we can't visit right now. Go back to your porch." I pulled back my hand and gave him the scoot-wave.

He responded with a sad look, but seemed to get the message, because he turned and wandered back in the direction of the house.

"You check the door," Clarence said. "If it's locked, meet me back here."

I nodded and slipped around the front, but when my hand fell on the knob, I hesitated. *Turn it,* I told myself. Then, again. *Turn it. Turn it. Turn it.*

I finally obeyed. The latch clicked free, and the door released. I swung it wide, but when I went to step in, I froze. The awful memory of being shackled in this place took hold of me, and my legs refused to move.

Luckily, the structure sat in front of the house with the entrance angled away from its view, so I remained hidden while I struggled to get hold of myself.

After too much time had passed, I heard Clarence say, "Psst." He was peering around the corner, giving me a questioning look.

I managed to summon enough strength to break free and push through the doorway.

The hens clucked at the sound of my footsteps as I edged along the threshold on weak knees. Reminding myself to breathe, I leaned against the wall and took in my surroundings.

The floorboards I had pried out had been reattached, with a fresh piece added in place of the one I had broken, concealing the skeletons once again. The replacement floorboard had another U-bolt and chain attached, ready for the next captive.

Clarence followed me in and gently closed the door behind him, avoiding a bang. "You okay, Missy?" He spoke in a low voice, switching his eyes between me and the chain.

I sucked in a shaky breath and nodded.

"Try not to think about it," he said. He went over to the window and peered out.

When I followed his cue, I saw Sonny through the hazy pane, back on the porch. There was no one else in sight.

Clarence checked his watch. "It's 9:40. Eli should be coming soon. Let's get ready." He took the box from me and held out the shotgun.

The weight of the gun in my hands brought the details of our plan back to me. I headed toward the door of the coop, and when I pulled it open, the hens sang out, *Bawwwk...bawk bawk bawk...bawwwk.*

"Sorry, ladies," I whispered. "Not yet."

The hens parted, clearing a path for me as I slipped inside. I pulled the door partway closed, far enough to block the chickens' exit, but wide enough to point the shotgun barrel through.

The hens rearranged themselves around me and returned to silence. I shifted into a spot that gave me line of sight to the outside doorway. Clarence rustled around as he got situated behind the bags of chicken feed, but from my position, I couldn't see him. After a minute, everything went quiet.

My heartbeat pounded in my temples. With my legs feeling weak, I locked my knees and told myself it wouldn't be long. I kept my mind occupied by playing through the details of our plan.

I wasn't sure how much time passed, but when I started questioning how much longer I could stand there, I heard the screen door slam.

"Is that him?" Clarence asked in a whisper.

"Yes," I said, raising the gun and pointing it at the doorway. My hands trembled, so I leaned the barrel against the doorjamb to steady it.

I counted the seconds, and when I reached twenty, the door swung out. I moved my finger to the trigger. Two arms reached in—I immediately recognized them as Eli's, placing a metal bucket and the wire egg basket on the floor. A shiny bolt held the bucket's handle, where it had been repaired.

The opening darkened as Eli stepped into the doorframe. With the bright outside light silhouetting him, my eyes took a moment to adjust. When they did, I saw his head was wrapped in a bandage. On reflex, I gasped at the sight of him. He must have heard me, because he shot a glance my way and went stiff. His eyes settled on me, then darted over to the corner where Clarence was hiding.

I heard the *thwack* sound of the arrow sinking into meat, along with the twang of the bowstring.

Eli flinched and grunted. When I saw the arrow sticking out of his bicep, I thought, *For real?* After Clarence had bragged about what a great shot he was, he'd been way off the mark at point-blank range.

Eli staggered backward, kicking the wire basket and sending it spinning across the floor. He bumped against the wall, staring in the direction of Clarence with wide eyes, as if trying to make sense of it all.

Everything froze for the next few seconds, which seemed like an eternity. Then, Eli straightened up with that arrow jutting out of his arm and a blood stain seeping through the fabric of his shirt. I damn near fired the shotgun, but a voice inside my head screamed, *Not yet!*

I heard the thwack sound once more. This time, Clarence's shot embedded right in the middle of Eli's torso. He let out a moan, his legs buckled, and he dropped to his knees with a look of disbelief painted on his face.

When his eyes locked on mine, he gave an almost imperceptible nod, which I took to mean, *Yeah, I deserved this.* I can't say for sure that's what he was conveying, though. It's entirely possible I was projecting that message onto him.

I expected Eli to collapse, but he didn't. A growing red stain encircled the arrow, but it dawned on me that it was a little below where his heart would be. I re-sighted the shotgun.

Eli groaned and turned his eyes to Clarence.

I heard Clarence's footsteps as he came closer. "Say your last prayer, you bastard." His words came out in a growl.

Eli's head tilted back as he tracked Clarence moving closer. Then, Clarence appeared in my narrow field of view through the nearly closed door, the bow fully drawn, the arrow aimed at Eli.

"Take their tongue," Eli said, straining to spit out each word. "Their lives are in the tongue."

Thwack.

Eli jerked when the third arrow embedded in his chest, a few inches above the last. He tottered, then collapsed onto his side. I let out the breath I'd been holding and leaned against the doorframe.

As I lowered the shotgun, I watched Eli for movement. He was as still as a rag doll.

"I almost pulled the trigger," I said to Clarence through the opening.

He turned around to face me. "Good thing you didn't. If you had, Bertha would be popping in right about now."

I stuck my head into the vestibule. "If you had taken any longer to get off that second shot, I would have fired."

"He gave me just enough time. I reckon I'm not as steady a shot as I once was."

No kidding, I thought, but instead of saying it, I said, "Your third shot was dead-on, though."

"Emphasis on *dead,*" Clarence said, nudging Eli with one boot, much like he had done to the wolves.

Without taking my eyes off Eli, I squeezed into the vestibule and closed the door behind me.

Eli made no sound and never moved. But my mind flashed back to how I had left him for dead when I broke free, and yet he'd recovered.

As if reading my thoughts, Clarence stooped down and put his fingers on Eli's neck. I looked on with my teeth clenched, ready to bash the man with the butt of the shotgun if he so much as twitched.

Half a minute later, Clarence stood back up and announced, "Dead as a doornail."

"Too bad he didn't suffer," I said, but I felt a smidgen of guilt for saying it. Yeah, this man had knocked me out and held me captive, but deep down inside, I understood he wasn't the one calling the shots.

They were.

But still. I'd watched a man die...killed by another person. I felt more numb than anything.

"Yeah, too bad," Clarence said as he disassembled his bow and packed it into the wooden case. "Just wish I hadn't wasted three arrows on him. I only got three left."

"Can you take these back?" I asked, gesturing to the ones sticking out of Eli.

Clarence shook his head as he snapped closed the steel tabs on the case. "They're barbed. I ain't cutting them out."

My mind flashed back to the memory of Clarence digging buckshot out of my body. I shuddered, knowing how much worse it would be to cut arrows out of a corpse.

We sidestepped Eli on the way to the door, pausing to look him over. "Her familiars didn't put up much of a fight," Clarence said.

"They didn't stand a chance against us," I said with a forced grin, although in my tense and fever-weakened state, I didn't feel all that powerful.

Clarence smiled back, flashing his pearly dentures, but his smile soon faded. His face went solemn as he picked up his bow case before saying, "Now, for the hard part."

Chapter 26

As Clarence slipped outside, I stopped in my tracks, taking one last look at Eli.

His mouth hung open, exposing the few remaining brown teeth.

I nudged his bandaged head with my foot. It rolled, settling at an unnatural angle from his neck. He was dead, alright. For this, I felt relief, but it wasn't so much a revenge thing. I felt more pity than hatred toward the guy.

Even so, didn't Eli deserve some blame in all this? He played along, and he had to know how wrong it all was. Hell, maybe we even did the old man a favor, finally freeing him from his lifetime of evil servitude.

Anyway, what mattered most was that this son of a bitch would never again support the heinous doings he'd been aiding for decades.

Clarence waited for me on the side of the henhouse where he stashed the gas can. He signaled for me to go first, so I led the way down the path the chanting procession had taken into the woods.

Along the way, I kept a lookout to ensure we were well hidden from the house. We passed the clearing with the fire pit and the area where I had lain in hiding to watch the ritual, before getting clubbed. I tried putting it out of my mind, but being right there made it tough.

When I reached the edge of the brush, I held up to wait for Clarence.

With him at my side, I pointed beyond the garden at the outhouse, sitting behind the home. He nodded.

Without a word, I scurried across the short clearing and squeezed between the cornrows, which I followed to the opposite end of the garden. Through the stalks, I caught glimpses of the back of the house and the outhouse.

Clarence arrived shortly after me at the end. He dropped to his knees, opened the wooden case, and went about reassembling the bow. I studied the three remaining arrows, amazed by the lethal look of the arrowheads, their barbs formed with razor-sharp steel.

He climbed to his feet, picked up the fuel can, and whispered, "Wish me luck."

I held up my crossed fingers and leaned back into the cornstalks so he could squeeze past.

He hunched, hurried across the grass with the fuel can in tow, and ducked behind the privy.

For the first time, I considered the possibility that someone might be using the outhouse. No problem if it were Bertha, but if it were one of my brothers, that would be a different story. I pushed the possibility out of my mind.

With both fists pressed against my mouth, I nervously watched Clarence. He spun off the SOHIO can's pour spout lid, lifted the can, and splashed its contents over the back of the structure.

The kerosene dripped down into the latrine cleanout along the back, which I realized meant flames would soon erupt through the toilet seat opening inside. The idea that one of my brothers was inside crept back into my mind, but I told myself not to worry. They would have heard Clarence and smelled the fuel, for sure.

When the can was empty, Clarence dropped it onto the grass, replaced the lid, and fished a box of matches out from his overalls' bib pocket. He struck a match and brought it to the siding. The flame expanded and spread across the back of the outhouse.

After grabbing the can, he ran back to our hiding spot and picked up the bow. As he notched an arrow, I noticed a strained look on his face and recognized a flicker of fear in his eyes. That crack in his mask of bravery dialed up my anxiety level even further.

We waited and watched in silence.

As the flames spread over the privy, I started to feel the heat, even from our safe distance. Soon, crackling sounds emanated from the inferno while a plume of smoke swirled into the sky, a sign that the aged wood was now burning on its own.

Our intent was for the fire to lure Bertha out of the house, where we would ambush her. But as I watched the flames stretch into the sky, for the first time, a terrible possibility crossed my mind.

Could the fire leap from the privy to the house? I eyed the distance between them, measuring it in my head. It was not much longer than the length of Clarence's truck. If the house were to catch fire, my brothers would be at risk. Why hadn't we considered this?

As the flames grew, I began questioning how long it would take for Ungodly to notice the fire. Could this be another flaw in our plan?

As if in response to my latest worry, Sonny appeared at the opposite side of the house, apparently drawn by his canine super-hearing. He stared at the burning outhouse for a moment, then barked. Soon, he was barking frantically, and it wasn't long before the home's rear screen door swung open.

Bertha stormed out onto the walkway and locked her enraged yellow eyes on the fire. The screen door slammed behind her.

Sonny immediately quit barking and slunk off with his tail between his legs.

I shook as I released the shotgun's safety. It wasn't just my hands; my whole body was quaking. Fighting to steady myself, I leveled the barrel with my finger on the front trigger and trained the shotgun's sights on her chest.

I heard the twang of the bow when Clarence released it. But the whoosh that followed ended with a solid thud, which I instinctively knew wasn't the sound of the arrow hitting flesh.

Clarence mumbled, "Dad-blasted."

Oh, my God, I thought. *He hit the house!* I wanted to scream.

But our plan was for me to fire as soon as Clarence took a shot, so I focused on lining up the sights and then started applying pressure to the trigger.

Of course, Bertha had heard the impact of the arrow behind her, and she whipped around right before I fired.

Boom! The percussive blast disoriented me for a moment. All I knew was that she didn't fall. I hurried to reposition myself and move my finger to the second trigger.

Bertha looked our way. We had to be well hidden in the corn stand, but for all I knew, she might've spied us with infrared eyesight.

In a flash, she was coming at us, circling clear of the burning outhouse, but moving inhumanly fast, like the way she had two days prior, when she bolted toward me inside the house.

And that scream... The horrid sound rose in a deafening chorus.

I fought the urge to drop the gun, cover my ears, and flee. Knowing there was no way I could outrun the hideous thing coming our way, I held my ground and raised the gun.

By the time I had her back in my sights, Clarence got off his next shot. The sounds came in quick succession: *Twang. Whoosh. Thwack.*

I immediately recognized the thwack as the sound of the arrow sinking into meat.

Bertha came to a screeching halt ten feet from us, with the arrow sticking out of her long dress in the area of her thigh. As she looked down, her scream crescendoed into an ear-splitting roar.

Before she had a chance to move again, I pulled the second trigger. *Boom!*

The sound cut off the scream as Bertha jerked back and folded over, telling me she'd been hit. It was a good thing, too, because now, my double-barreled shotgun had to be reloaded.

Bertha straightened up to examine her gut, where shredded parts of her apron encircled a spreading bloodstain. Still standing, she turned and yelled something in Pennsylvania Dutch over her shoulder.

As I reached into my pocket to retrieve the two other rounds, a wave of heat from the growing fire hit me. The cornstalks writhed around us. I turned and covered my face to shield it from the blast of hot air. Clarence grabbed me by the shirt and pulled me back.

After we retreated to a safer distance further down the row, I returned to the task of reloading the shotgun. I released the barrel lever as Clarence had shown me, hinged the barrel open, and shook out the two spent casings. With quivering fingers, I stuck the two fresh shells into the open chambers, swung the barrel up, and snapped it into place.

Just then, the back door of the house flew open. My heart sank when a barefoot Xavier stepped out, followed by Dustin, putting them in the line of fire behind Bertha.

But things went from bad to worse when I noticed my brothers both held guns.

Bertha staggered aside, clearing a path between the boys and us. She pointed our way and called something in Pennsylvania Dutch using a commanding tone.

Twang. Woosh. Thwack.

"No!" I cried, unable to believe that Clarence had taken a shot with my brothers in the line of fire.

The arrow had hit a body. Whose body?

It was Bertha who flinched, though. She steadied herself, then began to waver, before falling to her knees. Her hands clutched Clarence's last remaining arrow, now protruding from the middle of her chest, while blood seeped into the fabric of her apron like an expanding ink blot.

"Bullseye," Clarence said with a smug tone.

I wanted to hug him. He had made the perfect shot. When the stakes had been highest, he found his form.

The twins lined up side by side and began raising their guns. I lowered mine.

Clarence grabbed my arm and yanked me back. As he dragged me down the cornrow, I dropped the shotgun, but I left it on the ground. There was no one left I could use it on anyway.

Boom! Boom! The double shots tore through the cornstalks behind us—right where we had been standing.

When Clarence stopped at the far end, I damn near plowed him over. He pointed into the trees. "Let's cut through the woods and go around the chicken coop," he whispered. "We'll sneak up on them from the other side of the house."

As I gave him a thumbs-up, two more shots rang out. We bolted across the short clearing and into the trees. I figured my brothers wouldn't be able to see us from where they stood, with the back of the garden blocking their view.

Although we ran through the woods as quietly as we could, twigs snapped several times. I prayed the crackling sounds of the fire would cover up our noise.

When we passed the clearing with the fire pit, two more shots rang out.

"Nothing whizzed this way," I whispered to Clarence.

He shrugged. "Seems they're still firing into the cornrows."

We followed the trail to where it ended between the barn and the chicken coop. After circling the henhouse, I leaned against the front to catch my breath. Clarence took his handkerchief out of his bib pocket and wiped his forehead.

When I peeked around the corner, I saw that flames were now covering the entire outhouse, sending a thick trail of smoke into the sky. Bertha remained on her knees where she had fallen, still upright, facing away.

I spotted my brothers in the garden with their backs toward us, poking into the cornrows where we had previously been hiding. *Good thing you guys are dumb-asses,* I thought.

Sonny was back on the porch. After giving way so Clarence could take a look, he signaled the route we would take past the front of the house.

I gave him an *okay* sign.

He pulled a knife from his pocket and opened it. "You hold off the boys while I deal with Bertha."

Happy to keep my distance from Ungodly, I nodded my agreement. But I left my knife in my pocket. Using it on my brothers wasn't an option. Anyway, I was confident I could handle them without it. I just had to keep them from shooting us long enough for Clarence to take care of Bertha.

With the knife clasped in his palm, Clarence took another peek around the corner. "They're still searching through the corn stand. Let's go." He took off without waiting for a response.

I followed him, running in a crouch toward the front porch. During that short trip across the open yard, the twins never turned around. Sonny watched us approach with his tail wagging. Avoiding eye contact, I passed him by.

With the house hiding us from view, Clarence held up, beckoning for me to take the lead. I headed down the opposite side, following the path I had taken when I fled after being shot.

Halfway there, I could hear the crackling fire, and when I crept up on the rear corner, I felt a blast of heat.

When I peeked behind the house, Bertha drew my gaze. Frozen in the same kneeling position, clutching the arrow in her chest with her mouth hanging open, her profile looked nothing like an elderly woman. She appeared to be *my age,* with smooth skin and a firm facial structure.

But from my angle, I couldn't see her eyes.

As if she sensed our presence, she began turning her head to face me. Clarence grabbed me by the shoulder and spun me around. "Don't look at her!"

I nodded. When I swung back, I looked past her. Still poking around the cornstalks, one of my brothers was visible. The other was nowhere to be seen.

Shielding my face from the blast of heat with my arm, I leaped out and dashed along the back of the house.

As I sprinted past Bertha, my brother, who was standing outside the cornrow, began pivoting toward me. It was Xavier. I ran hard, and before he had a chance to brace himself, I barreled into him, knocking him into the corn stand before crash landing on top of him.

Scrambling to my knees, I yanked the gun out of his hands and rolled away from his reach. Without getting up, I released the lever, pivoted the barrels open, and shook out the shells.

Xavier recovered from my tackle, and a split second before he lunged for me, I flung the shells into the garden. We wrestled for half a minute, and that's all it took for me to get him in a headlock. I was well-practiced at tussling with my brothers, and I still had the upper hand.

Bertha's feral scream tore through the countryside. I desperately wanted to cover my ears, but I couldn't let go of Xavier.

When I turned my eyes to her, I discovered it was Clarence she was screaming at. Her jaw hinged open, her tongue extended, twitching as she howled. As he closed in on her, holding his knife at the ready, her milky yellow eyes burned in a hateful glower.

Bertha pulled back her lips, baring her shark-like teeth, exposed to the gums. Without warning, she pitched forward and dove at his legs. For a heart-stopping moment, I thought she'd snatch him in her grasp. But he jumped back just in time, and she fell on the ground, her arms flailing in the air.

Suddenly, I felt something cold press against my temple. I looked up to see gunmetal black. Standing between cornstalks, Dustin looked down his shotgun barrel at me with those empty eyes.

I saw movement out of the corner of my eye. Dustin looked that way, freeing me to do the same. Clarence pounced on Bertha, grabbed her tongue, and with one rapid swipe, severed it. In a snap, her expression changed from hatred to shock, before dissolving into a lifeless stare.

At that moment, Xavier went slack under my arm, while the gun barrel slipped off my temple, and Dustin dropped like a sack of potatoes.

Clarence recoiled from Bertha, with his eyes fixed on the horrible, long tongue dangling in his hand. A look of revulsion spread over his face, as if he had just come to realize what he was holding. He hurled it into the grass and hopped backward.

Bertha fell onto her side with her eyes closed. Over the span of seconds, her appearance transformed. The strip of hair showing beneath her kapp went from brown to gray to white. The skin on her face paled, then blanched to ash, as it shriveled into a leathery mask. Her lips thinned, exposing her pointed teeth, which then shifted from white to yellow, and finally darkened to brown. Her eye sockets sank inward, and her entire body seemed to shrink and curl into itself, like a drying leaf.

I gasped out loud. Clarence turned to me with wide eyes and his jaw hanging open. We exchanged one of those "did you see that?" looks. Neither of us moved for a spell, as if we were stunned into paralysis.

All of a sudden, the burning outhouse collapsed, sending a surge of embers into the sky.

Moments later, Sonny appeared at the corner of the house, panting and wagging his tail.

Clarence tiptoed over to Bertha, prodded her with his boot, and backed away to watch for movement. When she remained still, he bent over and fished something out of her apron pocket. He held it up for me to see. It was the small pouch I had seen at the fireside ritual. We exchanged a knowing glance, and he tossed it into the grass between us, not far from that dreadful tongue. I needed both.

My attention shifted to Xavier, who was leaning limply against me, and Dustin, who had crumpled onto the ground, face down. Neither moved.

Were they out cold? Were they even alive?

"Xavier!" I nudged him, then reached over to give Dustin a shake. "Wake up, Dustin!"

I waited a long, breathless moment before Xavier shifted. A few seconds later, Dustin rolled onto his side, straightened his arm, and blinked his eyes open. They sparkled with life, with none of that hollow emptiness from before.

I fell onto both of them, wrapping one arm around each. They squirmed underneath me, and Dustin pushed me away, saying, "What are you doing?"

I leaned back on my heels and studied them.

Xavier rolled off my thigh and began wiping his hands over his face. Dustin pulled himself onto one elbow and started looking around, squinting, like he was trying to sort out the unexpected scene he found himself a part of.

Clarence grunted. When I looked his way, he was lifting Bertha's severed head off her body by the hair bun, with the knife grasped in his other hand. No blood dripped from the freshly cut neck, as if she had already been bled dry.

He carried the head a few steps toward the fire and tossed it underhand into the flames.

An anguished moan sounded, which seemed to be coming from all around us. A chorus of moans. It grew distant, then faded away, leaving only the crackling and popping sounds of the fire. I caught a whiff of a sour odor.

After folding his knife, Clarence slipped it into his pocket as he stepped back to Bertha's withered body. With another grunt, he hoisted it up from the ground. Her headless frame no longer resembled a young woman; it had the twisted, fragile look of a ninety-year-old woman's body. He gathered what remained of her in his arms, straightened with a groan, and moved toward the fire, hurling it in. *Wump.*

Clarence watched the flames for a moment before turning and wandering back our way.

I would have done a little celebration dance if I felt better. All I could do was smile. "Burned at the stake," I said.

He gave me a wide, jubilant grin. "Yeah. In the shithouse, where she belongs."

Sonny strolled over and began licking Dustin's face. Dustin pushed him away and sat up, rubbing his eyes. He looked around, opened his mouth to say something, then closed it. Instead, he reached for the dog and began petting him.

"His name's Sonny," I told him.

"He sort of looks like Bluey," Dustin said.

"He does. He's like an old-man version of Bluey."

Xavier pushed himself onto his knees. He squinted in bewilderment as he switched his eyes between the fire, Clarence, me, and the house.

Dustin took a good look at him and snorted. He turned to face me and asked, "Why's he dressed like that?"

Chapter 27

Clarence rolled to a stop where the gravel road passed the gully and killed the engine. Without saying a word, he pushed open his door and slid out.

I did the same, then waited for my brothers to shimmy across the bench seat and climb down beside me.

It was good to see them wearing their own clothes, although they'd have to live with the haircuts for a while. They were acting themselves again, too, including their cringeworthy argument over who sat where. Hopefully, Clarence hadn't picked up on the fact that neither wanted to sit up against him on the tightly packed seat.

Sonny whined from the truck bed. Clarence headed over, then petted his head. "No, you're sticking with me, boy."

I felt my throat tighten as I circled the front of the Studebaker. I tried to swallow it away while I reached out to give Sonny a petting of my own. "Sorry, Sonny. Mom would kill us if we brought back another dog."

I turned my eyes to Clarence. "Are you sure you don't want to come with us?"

He smiled and gave Sonny one more head pat before turning to face me. "I'm an old man, Emma. An old-fashioned old man. I ain't cut out for life in your day."

I knew Clarence was being sincere about that. He had barely asked me anything about life in 2025—as if he didn't even want to know.

He lowered his gaze to the gravel roadway and kicked a stone to the side. "Plus, this might not work. You might be stuck here."

"No offense, but I hope not. Our dad needs us."

Clarence frowned and nodded.

"Do you do hugs?" I asked, doubting it was much of a thing in 1955.

He sighed and opened his arms. For the first time, I noticed his eyes were welling up with tears, and that was all it took. I broke down crying as I wrapped my arms around him. He squeezed me back, and we held each other in a long embrace.

When I finally pulled away, my brothers had taken over the stone-kicking act, only they were aiming at each other.

I wiped my cheeks dry. "Thanks for everything."

Clarence deflected it with a headshake.

"I mean it," I added, thinking about how he was the only other living soul in the entire valley. "If you hadn't helped me, I wouldn't be here." I pulled my brothers into a roughhouse-style hug. "Because you saved me, I could save my brothers. No... *We* saved my brothers."

Clarence grinned. "We made a good team."

I released my brothers and flexed a bicep, even though I didn't feel strong in my fever-weakened state. "We were *amazing.*"

"No more Bertha," he added. "And that's all because of you. So, no, thank *you.* All of Homer County is much obliged."

I felt my face turning red, so I spun around to face the gully.

"My sisters can rest now," Clarence said.

"And the other twins," I added, turning back to face him. "They're all free. Their souls have been released."

Clarence raised a finger in the air. "There's one more thing. Now I know what happened to my sisters. It's a small comfort, but you gave me closure on that. So, triple thanks."

I blinked, unable to respond. What could I say?

Clarence stepped inside the driver's door. "You won't forget about me, will ya, Missy?"

I felt another round of tears coming on, but I fought it back. "Seriously?" My voice came out squeaky. "After what we just experienced?"

He chuckled and climbed up onto the seat. "Holy Moly...you've got a point there."

As he fired up the truck, he leaned out the open window. "Remember, I'll circle back here after I feed the Yoder's hens and check on the rest of their livestock. If you have any problems going back, meet me here." He checked his watch. "I'll come by within the hour."

I gave him a dismissive wave, like trying to imply it couldn't possibly turn out that way. I'm not sure who I was trying to convince: Clarence, my brothers, or myself. Maybe all of the above.

After herding the twins over to the ditch near the gully opening, we waited there while Clarence pulled forward to start a three-point turn.

"His truck's a she," I told them while Clarence backed up to turn around. "He calls her Trotter."

"What do you mean?" they asked in perfect identical-twin unison.

I shook my head, unsure why I had even mentioned it. I guess I just felt I should say *something* to fill the silence. "I'll explain later. We'll have plenty of time for that."

The tires sprayed gravel as Trotter headed off in the direction from where we'd come. As he rolled past us, Clarence held his open hand up in a wave.

We all waved back. "He might seem like an old country bumpkin," I said, "But that's one bad-ass dude."

"Emma?" It was Dustin, the sound of worry in his voice. He was pointing down the road.

When I looked that way, my heart jumped into my throat.

A wolf.

Running toward us.

A wolf we had left for dead.

"Clarence!" I yelled, waving my arms.

With the truck obscured by its expanding plume of road dust, I realized he might not see me. And with the engine revving and the sound of gravel crunching under the tires, he may not have heard me either.

"Clarence!" I yelled again, although if he hadn't heard me the first time, the second time was hopeless.

All I could do was watch. My pulse fired like a machine gun.

Bearing down on us at a full sprint, the wolf shifted from the center of the road to our side. She drew closer and grew larger with each pace.

As the pickup sped up, it drifted from the center of the road to the opposite side. It seemed as though Clarence had seen the wolf and was giving it clearance. *So, this is how it ends?* went through my mind. *After all that, it ends like* this?

We had nothing to stop that wolf barreling toward us, and we had no weapons to defend ourselves. I grabbed my brothers and blurted out, "Run!"

But at the last moment, the truck swerved, fishtailing across the road and veering into the wolf's path. I heard a thump.

The pickup skidded to a stop, spreading a cloud of dust across the roadway, hiding the scene.

Dragging the boys backward into the gully, I held up right before the embankment blocked our view.

I heard the truck idling in the distance, but I could see practically nothing through the haze hanging in the air.

Bang. A shotgun blast rang out, echoing through the valley. A flock of black birds took flight from the trees behind us.

The dust cloud began to thin, exposing fragments of movement. Seconds ticked by, and as the air cleared, the image of Clarence formed, moving behind his truck, his back toward us. A furry mass lay on the road behind him.

Facing away, Clarence rested the shotgun over the edge of the truck bed while Sonny stood back and watched. Clarence leaned over and sighted down the barrel.

Something moved further down the road. There was still too much dust for me to identify it, but it wasn't hard to guess that the second wolf was coming, too.

Bang. The dark blur fell in a tumble.

Time stood still, with nothing moving. After a while, Clarence turned around to face us. He lifted the shotgun above his head and triumphantly jabbed the sky with it.

I raised both fists in the air and hooted, and soon, my brothers joined in the celebration.

After another round of goodbye waves, this time from a distance, Clarence drove off, leaving the wolf carcasses on the side of the road, where he had dragged them.

We lingered well after the sound of crunching gravel had faded out of earshot and the last of the road dust cloud had cleared.

With a deep breath, I turned around to lead the way on our trek along the gully, keeping one step ahead of my brothers so they wouldn't see the fresh tears welling up in my eyes.

"When are you going to tell us what happened?" Dustin asked from behind me.

"You guys don't remember *anything?*"

Without hesitation, he said, "No."

I glanced over my shoulder in time to see Xavier rub the side of his head as if he was thinking hard, before saying, "Me neither."

Considering it had taken me an hour or more to tell Clarence what I'd been through, I wondered if there was some way I could summarize it. But each detail seemed important, and right now, I was too weary to account for them all.

Besides, at that moment, the most important thing was finding our way back to our campsite and back to the era we belonged in. Then, if we could manage to do that, I had other things to tend to.

I held up and turned to face them. "I'm still trying to wrap my head around everything. Give me some time, okay?"

Neither pushed back, which made me wonder if they were still suffering aftereffects from being spell-bound. Like a hangover of sorts. Either way, I figured they'd be asking again before long.

"Plus, I need to pay attention to the path," I added as I continued leading the way along the ravine. This much was true because the route we were taking required hopscotching from side to side and over rocks large enough to stick out of the water.

Before long, I heard the waterfall, and a short time later, I saw it. Perched on the side of the gorge above us sat the viewing platform. A long rope dangled underneath, stretching all the way to where we stood.

"So, that's how you got down," I said, pointing at the rope.

Xavier gave me a blank stare, while Dustin just shrugged.

I went first. Fortunately, the embankment wasn't nearly vertical, so while the rope wasn't entirely necessary, it made the climb easier. But still, the aspirin was wearing off, so I was already in a fever-induced sweat before I even started. Feeling as crappy as I did, the climb was a grind.

The boys cheered when I grabbed hold of the platform. I tried to look strong, responding with a fist pump, but I had to lie down to recover while I waited for them to take their turns. I barely registered their back-and-forth banter down below.

When Xavier reached the structure, he climbed up and stood over me. "Are you okay?"

I nodded. "Just tired."

"What's that?"

I looked down at where he was pointing. The bullseye rash.

I couldn't believe he had noticed, since my brothers weren't exactly the most observant people I knew. "Just a bruise," I said, rolling over to hide it. "I bumped into something."

I stayed where I was while Dustin ascended, only making myself sit up when he arrived.

The strain of getting back on my feet left me feeling lightheaded, so I had to lean on the railing until the worst of it passed.

"This way," I said as I led us off the platform, telling myself, *You're over halfway there.*

A lightly worn path took us through the woods, which I hadn't noticed when I rushed through at night. After following it for a few minutes, I spied a clearing ahead. When we arrived, the pond came into view. Edged with cattails, it was free of duckweed. Even from where we stood, I could see there were no tents on the other side.

I walked into the clearing, and when I drew in on the bank, a dozen frogs plopped into the water.

My brothers lined up on either side of me and stared at the water hole.

Xavier said, "I remember this pond."

"Me too," Dustin said. He pointed at the flat area in the clearing on the other side. Tall grass covered the surface, but otherwise, it was empty. "We pitched our tents over there."

"That's right," I said. "But this isn't just any old pond." I dug Bertha's linen pouch out of my pocket. I also pressed against my other pocket, making sure I still felt its contents.

I untied the pouch's drawstring, teased it open, and took a pinch of the substance. It felt like sawdust. Since I had no idea what it was, I didn't want to smell it. "This pond is like a time portal," I said, tossing the stuff into the water, then flicking the residue off my fingertips.

A fish rippled the surface, drawn to the disturbance that might have been a tasty insect, before flitting away. The water soon returned to glassy calmness.

Nothing happened, so I dumped the entire contents of the bag into my open palm and cast it in.

As I brushed my hands clean, I studied the water. Still, nothing happened. My heart began to sink.

But then, the surface began churning where I had tossed the potion. Bubbles formed, and the water swirled. The twins both let out a gasp. A patch of purple mist appeared, then spread in tendrils across the pond.

"We go through the pond to get back to our time." I dropped the empty pouch on the ground and offered each of my brothers a hand. "Are you ready?"

They both took my hands, but didn't budge. "What's that purple smoke?" Dustin asked.

The haze had reached the middle of the pond and continued to expand. "I don't know," I said. "But I saw that when I came through the last time, so I think it means it's going to work."

I stepped down the bank and into the mist-shrouded water, which came halfway up my shin. My brothers remained fixed in place, tugging against me.

"It won't hurt us," I said. I had no good reason to know this, but after all I'd been through, purple mist seemed innocuous. Plus, what mattered was getting back to the campsite.

They each took a tentative step into the water. I took another pace, bringing the water halfway up my thigh. They followed. With one more step, the water reached my belly button.

I let go of my brothers and leaned forward, pushing off the bottom toward the middle. I treaded water with my face veiled by that purple mist, waiting for them to catch up.

"What do we do now?" Dustin asked, floating right behind me.

"We need to go under," I said. "All at the same time. We'll swim a few strokes underwater, and that should take us to the middle."

Xavier nodded.

"Okay. On three," Dustin said. "One. Two. Three."

We all took a deep gulp of air, then dove in. The world went silent. The cool water felt good against my fever-heated body.

I was the first to pop out of the water, and when I did, I couldn't see. I wiped my fingers over my eyes, thinking I had gone blind. But when I looked up, I discovered the nearly full moon and a starlit sky. A shadow surfaced beside me. It was Dustin.

Next, Xavier shot out of the water, blowing out a burst of breath through the sheet of water running off his face, like a breaching whale.

As we all treaded water in the middle of the pond, both of my brothers looked around with wide eyes. The purple mist was gone, but duckweed covered the surface, except for the black holes where we had broken through.

I squinted, straining to get a view of the area where our tents would be. My biggest concern had been whether we'd return to the same time era we'd left, so the sight of the tents would be a huge relief. But all I could see were the cattails lining the pond. "C'mon," I said, dogpaddling in that direction.

As I got close enough to shore for my foot to reach the bottom, I spotted a gap in the cattails. Was it the path we had trampled? I could only pray that it was.

I lugged my way up the sloping bottom with water pouring off my body, into the gap, and when my line of sight aligned with where we had camped, our tents appeared.

Not only that, near the edge of the water, I caught a glimpse of moonlight glinting off the pistol, right where I had left it. "We're back!" I yelled over my shoulder. "We made it!"

My brothers were good swimmers, so I left them behind and grabbed both the handgun and the flashlight, which I also found poking out of the grass nearby.

I rushed up the bank. For one thing, being in the water had switched my fever from hot to chilled, so with chattering teeth, I was anxious to get the fire going.

But a more important thing was on my mind as I hurried across the field to our tents. We'd made it back in the same era. But how much time had passed at the campsite? Like, was it the same night we had left? I desperately hoped it was, because if four days had passed, as they had for me, my phone would be dead.

When I stumbled into the campsite, the glowing embers in the campfire pit gave me my answer.

CHAPTER 28

I WAITED LONG ENOUGH to make sure my brothers would be sound asleep, then slowly scooted across my sleeping bag. On my knees, I turned on my little LED tent light, opened my pocketknife, and unfolded the T-shirt to reveal what I had concealed inside—the thing I had carried in my shorts pocket.

Bertha's tongue.

The Ungodly.

My stomach lurched with a gag reflex. Nothing repelled me more...

...yet I knew its power.

My hands trembled, partly from my chills, but mostly from distress. I strained to steady them as I used my pocketknife to saw off a sliver, trying not to think about what I was cutting.

I thought back on the campfire story I had told my brothers, my short story, "The Troll Skull." Afterward, I considered how desperate people can do reckless things, and recklessness may not turn out well.

Except, if there's a chance...

I poked the stick through the slice of tongue, attempting to ignore its repulsive details—its gamey odor, the marbling of fat and meat, the cross-sectioned blood vessels.

Once I had the piece of tongue mounted, I averted my gaze and took deep breaths to collect myself. Then, I crawled out of the tent as quietly as a cat. The bullfrogs had returned to their chorus soon after we had left the pond, masking my sounds.

I sat cross-legged beside the fire and steered my roasting stick over the embers. *Like a disgusting marshmallow,* I thought, and that's what I decided I should think of it as. I rotated the stick to brown the morsel evenly.

Before long, fat dripped into the coals, sizzling.

It was ready. Was I?

I would never be.

But I had to be.

My whole body shook with the fear I felt about what I needed to do. But I had overcome the fear I felt in Ungodly's presence, so I knew I could conquer this.

I steered the stick toward my face and blew on the fragment. I picked it off, fought through the nausea, and brought it to my lips, breathing through my mouth to avoid smelling it. I opened my jaw and pushed the foul meat between my teeth, trying not to let my lips touch it.

I bit down, and some juice dribbled into my mouth. I tore off a little piece and chewed it, rolling it across my tongue.

I fully expected this horrid thing to taste awful, but as it turned out, it didn't. It tasted like beef. I guess that helped, just a little.

It wasn't a big slice, so I forced myself to eat it all, one small nibble at a time. It probably took me ten minutes, but it felt like ten hours.

When I finished, I washed it down with a swig of water from my canteen, pushed the roasting stick into the fire, and crawled back into my tent.

Inside, I wrapped up the rest of the tongue and told myself, *That part's done. Don't think about it anymore.*

I burrowed into the sleeping bag, lay my head down, and closed my eyes.

Epilogue

Now — One Month Later

I open the purple-stained paper towel and pick out the five blackberries, tossing them, one at a time, into the grass at the base of the headstone.

I scan the letters on the grave marker one more time:

Loving Husband and Devoted Wife

Clarence John Henry
July 19, 1875 – October 24, 1963

Beatrice "Bessie" Lorine Henry
March 28, 1877 – January 25, 1952

Feeling a sting in my eyes, I tear my gaze away and look across the vast field of headstones in the Moravian Village Cemetery, built in a sweep surrounding the tragic Moravian Massacre site.

I roll the paper towel up into a ball and hand it to Dad, who says, "So, he lived eight more years."

I run through the math in my head. "Yeah. He would have been 88 then. He was eighty years old when I met him, but looking at him, you would have never known it."

Dad passes me the paper bag, which I open and then turn over, scattering the handful of popcorn onto the grass. Jiffy Pop. The closest I could come to old-fashioned, bacon-grease-fried popcorn.

I turn to face Dad, noticing his face has filled out. Within days, his skeletal limbs had begun to bulk up, and now, even his face looks stronger. "So, that's what happened, Dad. You know the complete story now."

"Well, up until you went to sleep in your tent."

"Right, but you can guess what happened next."

He chews his lower lip. "So, when you woke up, that bullseye rash was gone?"

I raise my hands, palms up. "No sign of it whatsoever. No fever. No aches. Even the wounds on my arm and leg, and the scab on the back of my head...all gone."

He clears his throat and faces the headstone. "And then, when you got home, you fed me some of that tongue."

I take a deep inhale. "Tongue puree, you might call it."

"Gross."

"Don't complain, Dad. At least you didn't have to taste it."

He bobs his head and chuckles. "I'd bet it wasn't easy slipping that into my feeding tube bottle."

I nod. "You can say that again."

"You sure took a big chance for your old man, girl."

I shrug. "Call it a gut feeling. Some things only turn good or evil in the hands that wield them. So far, so good."

I try not to, but I can't help but give his eyes a quick inspection. There's no sign of yellow. How long will it be before I'm able to break the compulsion to check?

I hook a finger under the red ALS bracelet, stretch it, and peel it off my wrist.

Dad wraps an arm around me, and I lean into him, so grateful for his presence. "Besides," I add, "It was a chance worth taking."

Placing my hand on the headstone, I think about Clarence—the man my family owes everything to. Without him, my brothers and I would be gone, and my father would still be wasting away on his deathbed.

And I couldn't forget all those identical twins. An untold number of innocent victims, taken from their families, over a span of time stretching almost 140 years...maybe longer. If there could be a silver lining to such a monstrous loss, it was that their life, their youth, their health, and the essence of their unique healing powers had given us an unimaginable gift: a magical cure to one of the most dreadful conditions known to man.

I place the bracelet on Clarence's grave marker, orienting it so the words "Let's Find a Cure!" face me. We can only hope that someday, modern medicine will do just that.

"So, are we cured permanently?" Dad asks, jarring me out of my thoughts.

I sigh. "Well, that's the essential question. We've used a portion of that tongue. If we need more, the rest is in the freezer."

Dad stares way off in the distance for a while. "And if we do need more, what happens when we run out?"

I touch the bracelet, running a finger over the top edge, but I don't answer. I *can't* answer. I can't even think about that, even though he's asking the same question I've pondered for the past month.

We stand there in silence for a long stretch until Dad breaks it. "I've got an idea... What do you say the four of us do that Buckeye Trail hike next summer?"

I turn to him with my throat tightening and my eyes filling up with tears.

"I mean, if you're not too busy," he adds.

I close my eyes and begin to bawl. He wraps both arms around me, and I sob against his shoulder. He squeezes me tight, patting me on the back.

As tears roll down my cheeks, I tell him, "Dad, I wouldn't miss it for the world."

Acknowledgments

Although I have some familiarity with Amish culture and practices, I hope nobody will view this fictional story as a reliable source of information on the subject, and I hope I'll be forgiven for any shortcomings.

Thanks to the authors who shared their experience with or knowledge of corruption within Amish communities. The nonfiction books, *Out of Deception* by Nathan Miller, *Breakaway Amish* by Johnny Mast & Shawn Smucker, and *Renegade Amish* by Donald Kraybill, all triggered my imagination, leading to this book's dark tale. If you're interested in the subject, each of those books is a fascinating read, written by authors who have intimate knowledge of Amish culture and practices.

Thanks to my nephews, Brad and Greg, who let me take them on a backpacking trip when they were teenagers. They wanted to do the Appalachian Trail, but I insisted on the Buckeye Trail instead. We began our hike in Tuscarawas County, which is one of the real-life counties that inspired the fictional setting for this and my previous books, Homer County, Ohio. I'll never forget how loud those bullfrogs were the night we camped beside a duckweed-covered pond at the back of a Boy Scout camp.

The Buckeye Trail passes by where I live, so I often go on day hikes along sections of this underappreciated state (and national) treasure. Thanks to the many generations of volunteers who established and maintained the trail over the years. In their honor, the main character of this story is named after Emma "Grandma" Gatewood, a legendary founder of the Buckeye Trail. I recommend reading her fascinating story, well-documented in several biographies.

Thanks to my fellow Ohio horror author, Katherine Kerestman, for sharing her knowledge of the history of witchcraft folklore with me.

While writing is a solitary endeavor, the input of others plays a big role in helping me improve my books. I want to acknowledge the many contributors to this project.

I'll start with the members of my critique workshop: Kelly Griffiths, Sean Seebach, Ann O'Mara Heyward, Rami Ungar, Jonathan Mitchell, and Randall Drum. Portions of this book were reviewed in two of our workshops and improved through the suggestions of my trusty colleagues.

Thanks to Marnie Vinge for her developmental edit and for taking the time to share her advice on publishing. I feel bad for throwing her under the bus (see below).

Our fictional friend Clarence John Henry would say, "Much obliged" to my real-life friend, John Henry. As one of the most analytical people I know, John has a sharp eye for finding logical lapses while beta-reading my stories.

Thanks to author Bill Halpin, who, once upon a time, the Horror Writers Association assigned as my mentor. This poor guy probably never imagined he would still be reviewing my work five years and three books later. He must be thinking, "Hey, I never signed up for this!" I sure appreciate Bill's excellent storytelling instincts and his way of seeing things that others (including myself) overlook.

I appreciate the time and talents of my critique partners, Sean Seebach and Kelly Griffiths. I've learned a ton from them since we started working together. I'm lucky to have their help, and I value our friendship even more.

Kelly made me work extra hard on revisions to this book, which, for a spell, made me want to strangle her. However, by the time I eventually finished working through her many helpful suggestions, I was glad she pushed me like that.

My apologies to Sean and his family for what happened to Bowie in this story. I really did have honorable intentions when I first borrowed their pet's name. But then Marnie (see above) came along and...well, things took a turn for the worse. There's a reason they call it horror. So yeah, it's Marnie's fault. Indirectly. I hope Sean's kids won't hold it against her for long.

With all my love, a million thanks go to my wife, Mary, who happens to be the most kind-hearted person I've ever known. I'm only able to put my energy into being an author through her boundless love and support, for which I am eternally grateful.

Last, but not least, I'd like to thank you, my reader. Doing a mind meld with you through stories I've dreamt up, which you reconstruct in your own imagination, it's like magic. But without you on the other end of this amazing process, I'd be toiling away on a pointless creativity treadmill, never going anywhere. I'm grateful to have you with me on my storytelling journey. I hope you're having as much fun as I am!

ABOUT THE AUTHOR

A FANATIC OF ALL things dark and creepy, Neil Sater lives with his wife, Mary, in the Cleveland, Ohio area. They have two grown children and two grandchildren. Having spent his career doing other things, Neil is happy to be now finding time for writing.

Neil has written four supernatural mysteries, all set in Homer County, Ohio, a fictionalized county fashioned in his imagination from areas of Coshocton, Holmes, and Tuscarawas Counties:

Phantom Realm: The Haunting of Misery Mansion (2023)
Mercy Killing: The Haunting of Ghoul House (2024)
Atrocity: The Haunting of Moravian Village (2025)
The Ungodly: The Curse of Forgotten Valley (2026)

Sign up for Neil Sater's newsletter through his website:
https://authorsater.com/
Follow Neil Sater, author on Facebook:
https://www.facebook.com/AuthorSater/
Follow Neil Sater, author on Amazon:
https://www.amazon.com/author/sater

Printed in Dunstable, United Kingdom

79378683R00150